Luna v. Moon

Chasing
DAYLIGHT

KATIE CRADDOCK

FREILING
PUBLISHING

P.O. Box 1264
Warrenton, VA 20188

www.FreilingPublishing.com

ISBN: 978-1-956267-18-1

Printed in the United States of America

CONTENTS

CHAPTER 1

Luna V. Moon. That is my name. I have never known what the "V" stands for, but that was my life. I was technically thirteen years old, if you want to count the years I was alive on Earth, three if you do not. Yeah, my birthday is on Leap Year.

Anyway, let's jump right to the almost exciting part—just before my life changed forever. I was on someone's rooftop, gazing at the stars. It was almost time to go back. 4:40 A.M. I could stay nineteen more minutes. The stars seemed to know I was leaving soon. They twinkled goodbye. I wished I could stay longer, as I was sad to leave the sparkling stars, and the pearl-like moon. They were my family.

But do not take my sadness too seriously. Back then, I thought I was just like normal kids. I could travel five miles a second. I could survive almost anything. I could lift six tons. I could see every little detail for, about, ten miles I think? And I could hear every little noise for that distance, too.

And when I ran home across the rooftops of the city, like that night, it felt like flying.

I was what I guess you could call beautiful. I had soft, silk-like hair that looks like sunrays—not that I have ever seen the sun. That was just what Eva told me. She said I also had bright blue eyes like the sky. But that was what confused me. My eyes were blue, not black. And, the sky was black. Anyway, I had skin as pale as the moon. I was slender and graceful.

I was an orphan, in an orphanage. Even though the place looked like what I would imagine a business building would look like. And, I was the only kid. Weirdly, all the workers had always gone home when I was awake. Eva said they were asleep, but I mean, come on, what was up with that? Was I contagious or something?

Eva was slender, like me, but much older. She had jet-black hair. She had caramel colored eyes that seemed to melt when she was with me. She was like a mother to me. (*Like I ever had a mother.*)

Every day, Eva brought me chocolate milk. It was bitter, but it helped me sleep. She said that if I did not drink it, I would stay awake, and that ten years later I still would not have slept a wink. It was one of the only things to look forward to besides gazing at the stars. I leapt over the last rooftop, and slid into my window.

Right after I got in the room, Eva came. As usual, her eyes softened as they found my face. "Luna," she murmured. She looked tired, more tired than usual. "I had a bad day." Eva opened her arms and I ran towards her for a hug. She combed her fingers through my hair. That always made her feel better. After a while, she stopped, and a pained expression crossed her face for a moment. Eva looked at the clock and sighed. "Come on Luna, you are going to be late for bed."

Eva spun around and grabbed my shoulders so tightly that I could not move anywhere but forward. She opened the door and shoved us both through. I turned my head, trying to see what Eva rushed us away from. As I turned, I saw a light. Not moonlight. Not a flashlight or light bulb light. No, this was different. Clearer, brighter, purer. It was beautiful.

Eva hurriedly shut the door, and practically dragged me to the kitchen. There, on the table, sat my chocolate milk. Eva let go of me and rushed to the refrigerator. She took a carton of white powdery stuff, and poured it in my chocolate milk. Then she grabbed a spoon and mixed it in.

After she put the things away, she came over. "Well, drink up," Eva whispered as she softly shoved me towards the chocolate milk. Like I needed it. I quickly sat down and took my first sip. I almost spit it out. Eva, seeing me bug-eyed, swiftly rushed over. "Come on," she urged. "Just one more sip and then we are done." I swallowed one more sip, then almost collapsed. Eva caught me; I fell asleep.

CHAPTER 2

That night, like usual, I dreamt of nothing. Then I felt someone shaking me.

"Luna, come on, Mr. Shrude is here."

"Go away," I said, rolling in my covers. I did not want to be tested. Especially not this early.

"Luna," Eva groaned, her tone serious. She leaned next to my ear, and whispered as quietly as she could. "I will tell them about the rooftops," she threatened. I jumped up, suddenly energetic.

"You better not," I growled. She pretended not to hear me. I looked down, and saw that I was dressed in clean clothes. A black t-shirt and shorts. Figures.

Those rooftop visits were my only free time. Everybody left me alone, because I was supposed to be "playing" with the toys they gave me. Once, Eva caught me, but she promised not to tell as long as I did not get into trouble. As soon as I walked near the door, I heard *his* voice in the hallway. It was a sound that never failed to chill me to the core.

"Okay, Eva," Mr. Shrude called out, "I think today we should probably start with the Disaster-Master."

Mr. Shrude was a big man, with broad shoulders and a voice that can make almost anyone listen. He was a little gruff, and not that strong. He can pick up only three hundred pounds I think. Every couple of days he came, and I had to show him my skills. He wrote it down, and then went away. The whole process took almost the whole day.

Eva flinched at his suggestion. The Disaster-Master gave me a lot of pain, both physically and mentally. The goal was to see if I could survive. Every time I tried it, they ramped up the power from last time.

Mr. Shrude did not wait to see if I would follow him. Instead, he flung me out of my room, and into the hallway. My back slammed into the metal wall, and the wall gave way a little. My back stinging, I felt the wall behind me and looked down. Yeah, another dent. The wall in front of my bedroom was full of them from all the times he had flung me in the past.

I tried to stand up, and cringed from my prickling back. If I did not get up, he would fling me to the next wall. Mr. Shrude's eyes were on the clipboard, and he scribbled furiously. Once he finished, he stood up straight and tall, as if the tuxedo he wore made him more important than everyone else.

He scanned the wall for me. I was up now, rubbing the back of my head. When his laser-beam eyes found me, he growled, "Come on, I don't have all night. Ahem ... day, day." He corrected himself quickly, trying to cover up his mistake. *Why in the world would he say night? Was it not daytime? And what was that mysterious light?* These questions all flew through my head at the blink of an eye.

We walked. I looked at Mr. Shrude's face. His skin was light brown. His face was cold and hard. I look at my own hand. It was as pale as the moon. *Did I have a normal childhood? Was I a normal child?* As my regular doubts played tag, I looked at Eva. She had the same skin as me. She was graceful and slender like me. *And, she was normal ... right?*

We turned left and... walked. Finally, in the too familiar hallway, we turned right. There was a white door that almost blended with the wall. "Go in," Mr. Shrude commanded, an almost excited expression on his ever cold face. I hesitated. *What were they going to do to me this time? Shoot bullets at me? Dump me in a tub of acid? Make me have a cage fight with a tiger? Throw fire at me?*

Eva saw I was distraught, but offered no words of encouragement. Instead, she muttered, "I will be going now," turned, and raced down the hall. I heard the jangle of keys, and the opening and closing of a door. Probably the cell. It's a jail cell where they put me if I didn't behave. My ears made out a click. Mr. Shrude huffed in annoyance, then opened the door.

"Come on," he growled. Trembling, I stepped through.

The Disaster-Master had a single square room with metal walls. It was empty except for a single chair in the center. Across from the chair, a clear window let Mr. Shrude, and sometimes others, watch me. I could not see much on the other side, but I could see the lights of blinking control panels.

As I walked towards the all too familiar metal chair, I braced myself. The chair was scarred and burned from tests and experiments. I sat down, and buckled in. Not too loose, but not too tight. Perfect for getaways.

When I finished buckling myself in, a plate rose up next to me from the ground. It had a red sponge.

"Squeeze the sponge," the attendant ordered through the loudspeaker. I looked towards them and saw Mr. Shrude giving me a weird creepy sneer. Probably as close as he would ever get to a smile.

I picked the sponge up. It definitely had liquid inside. I kept my hand and the sponge over the plate. I squeezed. A red liquid squirted out of the sponge. It fell on the plate and sprayed on my arm. My whole forearm and hand was covered with it. The strong stench of salt filled my nose. It smelled like blood. I didn't know *how* I knew what blood smelled like; I guess it was just something I was born knowing.

I dropped the sponge. "Eeeeewwwww!" I shrieked, shaking my right hand. "Eeww! Ew, ew, ew!" I started undoing my "seat belt." It was difficult, doing it with only one hand, but, finally, I freed myself. I took a quick peek at Mr. Shrude. He had an expression on his face that I had never seen before. It was… confusion.

I raced across the room, and tore the door down. As the door ripped from its hinges, I ran. And I ran to… the bathroom. Before you can even think, I was there. I ran so fast, the blood dried. I squirted soap all around my forearm. Then I put it under the faucet and scrubbed. I scrubbed and scrubbed until my skin was light pink and raw. As the flecks of blood went down the drain, I wondered: *Why would they do this to me? Where did they get the blood from?* I hoped no one was hurt.

Someone knocked on the door.

"Luna, are you okay?" It was Eva.

"Eva, that is the grossest thing I have ever seen! And I have seen *a lot* of disturbing things." I turned off the water and stormed off towards my room. Eva followed me.

"Luna, um, the good news is that Mr. Shrude wants a meeting with me to discuss what happened, so you're free. G-go out and do your stargazing, I need to go. No lessons today." Something was up with Eva, but I pretended not to notice.

"Okay, see you later," I said as I leaped out my window. I scurried up to the rooftop. Eva quietly opened and closed the door. I counted to five.

One Luna V. Moon. Two Luna V. Moon. Three Luna V. Moon. Four Luna V. Moon. Five Luna V. Moon.

Without making a sound, I climbed back into my room and, on tiptoe, I zoomed across. I opened the door and peeked outside, catching a glimpse of Eva just as she turned right. I followed her, keeping to the shadows. Once, Eva looked back, but she kept going.

Finally, we made it to the conference room. Eva went inside. She almost closed the door all the way, then thought twice, and left a crack open. Through the crack, I saw her sit down across Mr. Shrude.

"Okay, now, something really strange happened when we did the test," Mr. Shrude began. "Instead of lapping it up like her life depended on it, she looked at it in horror, started shaking her arm and screaming 'Ew! Ew!' As a Drinker, this is not normal." Eva turned paler than she was already at the word "Drinker."

"Yes, that is not normal for a Drinker," Eva replied. "And Luna is not normal like an H-B."

What? Drinker? H-B? What are they talking about? Definitely about me and the "incident" that happened today. Eva sounded like she wanted to cry.

"I-I should be going now." Eva got up, head down, looking defeated. She walked towards the door. I raced back to my room and sat on my bed, just in time for her to pop her head back in. "Come on Luna, let's go," she summoned.

I sprinted to the kitchen with Eva, wanting to drink my daily chocolate milk. Eva got out a glass, a carton of milk, chocolate, and the powdery stuff. She mixed the things in the glass, but she put in only one teaspoon of the powder, not two teaspoons like usual. Eva does not seem to notice. I drank my chocolate milk. It seemed… sweeter.

After I finished it, I returned to my room. I changed into a shimmery black t-shirt and shorts. They sparkled like the stars in the sky. I went over to my bed and laid down. As soon as my head hit the pillow, I was asleep.

The darkness overtook me. Someone shook me. It was probably Eva, so I ignored her. Soon she left me alone. In a couple of—what felt like minutes—Eva shook me again.

"Wake up! Luna, wake up!" she said sharply. "We have a lot to get through, and not much time to do it." In the middle of my room, there was a cart, with little test tubes and vials.

"Can we do this later? I have a very important appointment with sleep right now," I grouch.

Eva growls, annoyed. "Come on Luna, it's time for your blood draw!"

Groaning, I got out of bed, and Eva filled the vials with my blood.

"Well, it's almost one o'clock," Eva said, after I completed one of her grueling academic exercises five times. "Good-bye."

"Bye, Eva." I turned around, hopped out of my window, and was gone.

As I ran over the houses, I thought about the information from last night. *What were Drinkers and H-Bs?* I could not have heard wrong, so I have no clues, no leads on what they were. *What was happening to my life?* I mean, I was not complaining when I say that, because I was sick of my daily routine. Wake up, lessons with Eva unless Mr. Shrude came, and if he did, we did testing the whole day. Then, stargazing. After that, my chocolate milk. Then sleep. Repeat. Etcetera, etcetera. I finally sat down and made myself comfortable on someone's rooftop.

Just before I lay down, I thought I heard someone moving. I sat so still, you would think I was a statue. I heard it again. I was not imagining it. I carefully looked over the edge of the rooftop. I scanned the bushes, where I thought I heard the noise from. As I looked, I scanned past a pair of dark brown eyes. The eyes were so dark, they looked almost black; the irises mixed with the pupils of the eyes. As soon as I noticed them, I looked back immediately. The eyes were gone. Just to be safe though, I moved to the other side of the roof.

CHAPTER 3

I woke up with Eva standing over me. "Come on, sleepy head! Wake up! Today we are going to do some writing practice!" I groaned. I was horrible at writing. Eva pulled out some papers from a neat stack and put them gently on my rickety desk. If it was not for five rolls of duct tape, it would not even exist. In fact the table was more tape than desk. It was gray with flecks of old wood showing through. I got up and sat back down on a foldable chair. It was almost as unstable as my desk.

My clothes caught my eye. I sighed. This outfit was only supposed to be used when there was a laundry backup. Which there was. It was a neon pink t-shirt and shorts. I hated this outfit because I liked to stay in the shadows. Eva handed me my non-perfect pen. The pen was a nightmare. Either it gave so much ink that the ink went everywhere and almost destroyed my clothes if they were not washed right away (which I was fine with right now), or it gave so little ink that you could barely see the words I was writing.

"Okay, Luna, write what I say," Eva began. I took the cap off of my pen and straightened the papers on my desk.

"Yes ma'am," I sighed. It was going to be a long lesson.

I hate writing. I do not care. Get me out of here. Help. Blah blah blah. Boring. Too bored to be smart. I wrote absentmindedly. Just get to the point already Eva!

Eva peeked over my shoulder to look at my work.

"This is unacceptable young lady!" Eva shouted. "You will not be leaving this room until you have done what I have asked you to do! I suggest you get to work." Eva slammed more papers onto my desk (which shook so hard I thought it was going to fall on my feet), stomped over to my window, and took out a device from her pocket that I had not seen in a long time.

"WHAT!" I screamed. " YOU CANNOT DO THIS TO ME! IT IS AGAINST THE LAW!"

"What do you know about the law? You have not even memorized the whole multiplication table, much less the whole law! You need to finish *all* of this, but it is time for me to go. And if you take *one step* out of this room, *I will know!*"

CHAPTER 3

Eva shouted and shook the device clenched in her fist in the air. "And I *will* use this," she whispered. Her caramel eyes glowed in anger, like a blazing fire.

The device looked like a medium sized silver calculator with an antenna sticking out of the top. I eyed my right wrist. A tight, silver steel band was wrapped around it. As long as I had it on, they could track me. The device tracked the band, and I was not strong enough to tear the band off. It was too thick.

"Goodbye," Eva growled angrily. She left the room and slammed the door at the speed of lightning. I sat down, grumbling. Why was Eva suddenly Miss Perfect?

My thoughts were interrupted when I heard a quiet *Tha-bonk! Tha-bonk! Tha-bonk!* coming from my window. I quickly rushed over, surprised by what I saw. A girl. She looked like me, except with day-black hair and black eyes, twinkling like stars.

"Let me in! Please! I can help you! Luna, let me in! It's me! I've come back! It's me, Ivy! Ivy Moon, remember?" the girl whispered urgently.

Reluctantly, I let her in. This "Ivy" person climbed through the window, talking rapid fire.

"Luna, we got to go, like, right now if we are going to escape. Wait, where's Mom?" she whispered, glancing around the room. I slowly backed away from her, then tripped on a singing rowboat toy. Its annoying song filled the air.

"Love, love, love, always bring the love, like a river-rrrrrrr! Happy, happy, happy, always be happyyyyyy!" it squeaked. I fell. Ivy rolled her eyes.

"Ugh, those toys are sooo awful, don't you agree? It's like they think we're newborns." I stood up against the door, my left hand on the door-knob. My eyes were wide with fright.

"Okayyy," I drawled awkwardly, trying to keep my voice from trembling.

Hearing my awkwardness, Ivy laughed. "Yeah, I get it. It's kinda weird hanging with someone you haven't seen in a long time. But, you know, it's cool." *What? It's cold? What does that even mean?* Ivy seemed perfectly at ease with such a stranger. I turned the doorknob and opened the door. Just as I got it open a crack, she dove at me, whisper-shouting "No! What do you think you're doing? You're going to expose us!"

But it was too late. I heard Eva's footsteps down the hall. Ivy's terrified face told me she could hear them too. "You don't remember me," she despaired. Ivy turned around and went out the window. Before she dropped to the ground, her intense eyes bored into mine and she whispered,

"I'll be back, Sister. For now, just *don't* drink the chocolate milk."

Then she was gone.

CHAPTER 4

"I'm back." Eva stated the obvious. "Have you written the sentence fifty times yet?" She hadn't noticed the open window. So far, so good.

"No," I muttered. "I was busy." I could clearly see the rage in her eyes.

"Fine. We will do this tomorrow," Eva answered coolly. She stared into my face. "Luna, why does it feel windy in here?" she asked quietly. Darn. I guess it was too much to ask that she did not notice that a stranger was here AND that the window was open.

"Um… it was too hot?" Eva probably was not going to accept that.

"Luna V. Moon." Now I had done it. Eva does not use my full name unless she is steaming.

"I've seen you trudge across a 222°F simulation desert! I think you can stand a…" she looked at the thermometer above my desk. "70°F room. But I do not want to torture you. Come on. Let's go drink your chocolate milk."

✩ ✩ ✩

The next morning, as soon as I woke up, Eva came into my room. Behind her, I saw Ivy. Or did I? As Eva got closer, Ivy disappeared. "You're up early," Eva said worriedly.

"I just got up."

A look of relief spread across her face. It quickly passed. The same coldness took control, like it had before. She said just three words.

"Get. To. Work." Not hello, how are you, not even a smile. Just get to work. I sat down and started writing *I WILL write whatever Eva says.* With a few modifications.

> *I WILL write somethings.*
> *I WILL write somethings.*
> *I WILL write somethings.*
> *I WILL write somethings.*
> *I WILL write somethings.*
> *I WILL write somethings.*

I will not bore you with the rest of the forty four sentences. Anyway, when I FINALLY finished, I had a couple of minutes to stargaze. Naturally, like any person in their right mind would do, I opened my window and scrambled to the roof. Tonight I ran and visited The Chocolate Shop. I love chocolate. Even if just to stare at it. Or smell it through the window.

As I jogged, the wind whispered a message to me. *"Don't drink the milk,"* it said wistfully. As I was running past, a sign caught my eye. It said, "NO MILK! NO MILK for all you lactose intolerant! New and improved!" The leaves rustled in harmony with the wind. The trees swayed. *"Don't drink the milk! Don't drink the milk!"* they all sang. It seemed like everything was agreeing. It sounded like a chorus. *"Don't drink it!"* sang the altos. *"Don't drink the milk!"* the sopranos sang, but they all agreed, singing in harmony. I felt like the only one disagreeing, the rebel. The longer I was out there, the louder it got. More voices joined in. It got louder.

I reached The Chocolate Shop. I laid down and closed my eyes, hoping the voices would go away. They didn't. They only got louder. And louder. I tried to ignore it, but my defences were crumbling. I couldn't bear it any longer.

"Fine!" I shouted to the moon. "I'll do it!" The voices finally stopped. No more opera, no more screaming, no more nothing. Except silence. But there was one downfall. I had to do it. If I didn't, they would know. If I didn't, they would come back. The voices. They would haunt me until I did it. But, for now, I pushed that thought aside. I enjoyed the quiet. I soaked it all in. I looked at the sky. 4:59 A.M. Did I tell you I can tell the time just from looking at how light or dark the sky is? Anyway, I started home.

CHAPTER 5

E va looked tired. She tried not to show it, but that made me notice more.

"Let's go," she said, trying (and failing) to stifle a yawn. As we walked down to the kitchen, I thought about how to trick Eva. *Maybe I could... could... could what though?* She was smart, fast, and cunning. She was also not easily tricked. Eva's voice, like a knife, cut through my train of thought.

"Your milk is ready for you, in the kitchen. I have a meeting tonight, and every night for the next couple of months. I trust you'll be good." After I nodded, Eva opened the door and I went inside. After she closed the door, I heard a click. I was locked inside.

There was no way out.

☆☆☆

In the kitchen, there are no windows, doors, or secret passageways. Like I was going to escape anyway. The kitchen was a regular kitchen.

Refrigerator, oven, microwave, cabinets, pantries, drawers, chemical closets, that sort of thing. Plus counters and chairs of course.

I looked around, trying to find a place to put my chocolate milk where they could not find it. The sink? No, we did not have a disposal. The refrigerator? No, Eva looks in there every day. The potted plant? No … Hmm. Actually, that is not a bad idea.

I walked towards the plant in the corner of the white room with my chocolate milk. Sadly, I poured it into the pot. The soil soaked it in, as if it had never had anything so delicious in it's life. I took the empty glass and put it in the sink. When I sat down, Eva came in. I acted tired, so she would not suspect anything.

"Go to bed, sleepy head," she whispered.

"Okay," I mumbled "sleepily." I went out the door. Eva followed me out the door, turned the corner, and zipped off. When I could not hear her any longer, I raced off to my bedroom. I ran so fast that my feet barely touched the floor. It was like I was flying a few inches off the ground. In less than a millisecond, I was in my room.

I changed my clothes to my favorite shimmery black outfit. I sat on my bed, wondering what to do. I looked at the clock. 5:10 a.m. *Could I go outside?*

I looked at the window for no particular reason. A faint light was there. It might be the strange light I saw from yesterday. *Or... what was that?*

Timidly, I got out of bed and stared out the window. I was awestruck. I could not do anything but look with my mouth open. I think it was something called a sun... sun... sunrise? I believe Eva said something about it. That when the sun rises it is called a sunrise and when it sets it is called a sunset. Eva said that the sun is the moon of the night, but I never imagined it so bright.

Blinding pinks, glistening yellows, and a rainbow of colors I had never seen before. A ball of dark yellow was in the sky. And white fluffy things were in the sky too. I did not want to miss anything.

I was still at the edge of the window, so the light did not touch me. Timid, once again, I reached towards the light. My fingertips reached the light first. An incredible warmth that I had never felt before danced through my fingertips. Soon, my whole hand was in the mysterious light, enjoying its warmth.

Suddenly, my whole hand was burning. I jerked it out of the light, clutching it to my chest. I took a couple cautious steps backwards, horrified. After a few minutes, I took a step forward. Then another.

Then another. In no time at all, I was back where I started. For now, I was content just watching.

CHAPTER 6

A couple hours later, a bell rang. Noises I guessed were kids shouts stopped. Every time I looked towards a strange building, where the kids disappeared into, I saw them working. An adult was in front of them, teaching them from what I could guess. In one room I saw a girl with a brown ponytail and big brown eyes put a thumbtack on an adult's chair when the adult stepped out of the room for a minute ("Nice job Summer!" one girl whispered, giving the other girl a hand slap). In another room, I saw people working with some chemicals (one person mixed blue with yellow and it exploded in his face. I laughed quietly to myself). Through another window, I saw books. Millions and millions of books. I wanted to run into that room right then, because I only owned a couple of books. Tearing my eyes away from that scene, I looked through another window in that building. This one had technology. I did not know what it was called, but it was big, and had a screen and a keyboard. It also had, get this; a mouse. A dead mouse attached to it. It did not look like a mouse, from the pictures I had seen, but that is what Eva told me. It also had wires sticking out of it. I looked at every little detail, trying to put the puzzle pieces together. *What does this mean?*

A couple of hours later, the bell rang again. Everybody, except for the adults, came rushing out, big lumps strapped to their backs. They ran *(which was really slow. Do they really call that running?)* to their houses, panting from the effort. Or maybe from the heat. Strangely, they were laughing. I felt a strong yearning to be with them, instead of here. Alone. As they burst through their doors, a colorful leaf fell through my window. Only the edges were green. That meant it was… autumn? The center of the leaf was yellow with brown spots here and there. I threw it back out the window and watched it drift away.

A while later the moon came out. I hopped into bed and pulled up the covers. It had definitely been worth it, not drinking the chocolate milk. I had made up my mind. I was going to see the sunrise once more.

Eva came in.

"Wake up sleepy head," she called softly.

CHAPTER 6

☆☆☆

I slowly opened my eyes, trying to seem normal. "You better get up, Mr. Shrude is coming," Eva warned. I instantly got out of bed, not a second too soon. I heard Mr. Shrude's footsteps echoing down the hall. My back straightened automatically as he came in.

"Today is the muscle test," he said casually, finally glancing at me. I groaned inside. My muscles would be sore for days. "Well? Let's hop to it!" he said, feigning cheerfulness. His black tuxedo had not one speck on it.

We walked to the track first, in the gym. As Mr. Shrude pulled a timer out of his pocket, I routinely set up at the starting line. I was glad that he did not fling me into the wall today.

"2… 1… go!" I ran, but I was distracted, remembering the colors and the amazing sunrise. When I was done running one hundred laps around the track, Mr. Shrude stopped the watch. "Ten minutes? Seems like you were distracted Luna. Would you mind telling me what distracted you?" My heart raced.

"I was just thinking of an… idea for my muscles not to be as sore after today, that's all!" Mr. Shrude looked skeptical, but he accepted it. That was too close. We went into the next room. A basket was in the middle.

"We will start off with something easy. One ton," he said. I put the one ton weight in the basket and then picked it up. Slowly, Mr. Shrude told me to put more weights in until it was up to six tons and fifty pounds. It was so heavy, I almost dropped it. Then Mr. Shrude added a one pound ball. He stepped back. I dropped the basket. All the weights banged and clanked as they hit the floor. Oops. Mr. Shrude let out a frustrated sigh. "Fine. Just… just lift weights." So I lifted.

I lifted weights until Eva said "Luna. Come drink your milk."

☆☆☆

I lay down in bed. "Good night, Luna."

"Good night," I whispered as she left the room.

CHAPTER 7

As more nights passed, my yearning to be with the other children grew stronger. Finally, I couldn't stand it any longer. As Eva came in, I thought to myself, "It's going to happen. Tonight."

The day seemed to slug by. Everything was in slow motion. Only when I got to my room and put on my favorite outfit did things start to speed up. I grabbed all of my clothes and books, a water bottle, and a plain black cloak. I took one last look at my room. I had one last thing to do before I left.

I peeked into Mr. Shrude's room. If someone caught me I was dead. Luckily, no one was in the room. I found what I was looking for. A lumpy-strappy thing that I saw the children wear, and a pair of "socks and shoes." It's really weird. You put these... things on your feet. Why? I have no idea.

I stuffed in a sheet-like blanket that I took from my room (never know), and a hair tie that Eva gave me. It keeps the hair out of your eyes. Eva did not know about this trip though. AT ALL. I nearly jumped out of Mr. Shrude's window.

"Almost forgot," I muttered, as I pulled out a tiny silver key. I unlocked my wristband and put both the key and the cuff back into his desk. I rubbed my right wrist. It felt strange not to have my wristband on. I examined my arm. There was a really pink marking on my wrist where the band was. I was free. Almost. I jumped out of Mr. Shrude's window. His office was on the first floor, so I closed his window so no one would notice I was gone right away.

Finally, I raced into the light. I found a deserted and well hidden area near the strange building the children went into. I set up camp, thinking, but not noticing what I did with my supplies. I knew I had to go to the strange building so I wouldn't look out of place. The street was the first place Mr. Shrude would look. I also had to not draw too much attention to myself. So, I guess I had a plan.

Soon the bell rang in the building next to me. I "ran" (did it seem normal enough?) to a door I saw everybody walk into. Then I slowed to a walk. Since I had no idea what I was supposed to do, I asked someone.

I tapped a girl on the shoulder. She had shoulder-length black hair, and tan skin.

"Yes?" she asked, turning around.

"Um… my name is Luna, and I am new here. I was wondering if you could help me?" I asked her. She stood there, eyes wide, mouth open.

"I-I'm Janice. N-nice to me-meet you," she stuttered. Her eyes, from what I could tell, were hazel. "Uh, let's step out of the crush," she said, gesturing to a wall. As soon as we moved, a rush of children ran past us. "You see the door next to us?" Janice asked. The plaque outside the door said *Mrs. Fweep, Secretary*. "That's Fweep the Creep's office. The door across from her is Mr. Mean. He is actually quite nice. Well, anyway, just tell him you're new, then he'll ask a few questions. Answer them, he'll put you in your home room. Shoot, I have to go. See ya." Janice waved goodbye and dashed off. By this time, few stragglers were left in the hallway. I dodged them easily, then opened the door. He was on me immediately.

"Mrs. Fweep, get me a cup of coffee, will you? Decaf with whip, you know, the usual." The man looked over from his desk. "Oh, sorry, I thought you were my secretary." The man looked over me and his face fell with exasperation and tiredness. "What did you get in trouble for? Chewing gum? Throwing spitballs? Starting a food fight?" I cleared my throat.

"I'm new, Sir," I whispered.

"Oh! You're the new student!" he said, perking up immediately. The man had green eyes, shaggy brown hair, and was wearing a suit. "Well then. I'm Mr. Mean. And no, I'm not mean." Mr. Mean chuckled at his comment. "Anyhoo, what is your name? I'm the principal at this fine middle school." I stepped closer to Mr. Mean's desk.

"Luna, sir. Luna V. Moon." Mr. Mean took a piece of paper and a pen from his desk and wrote something down.

"What school did you come from, Luna?" he asked. I was in major trouble. I was a fake skol away from getting caught! So, I did what any other person in my position would do. I made up a skol.

"Larr... ing... ton?" I put together letters randomly and desperately.

"Mmm-hm. Good school, Larrington. How old are you?" I could not believe my luck! Larrington was an actual skol!

"Thirteen." I answered, relieved. Mr. Mean chortled.

"I was the smartest person in my whole school when I was your age."

"So this place is called a skol," I tried to say casually. Mr. Mean sighed and rolled his eyes.

"Kids these days," he muttered. "No. A school. S-c-h-o-o-l. Not skull. Scchhooaall." Mr. Mean said it slowly, like I was a little child. "Anywho, your homeroom teacher is Ms. Zooka. I'll walk you to your classroom." Janice was right. Mr. Mean was nice. At least, one of the nicest people I had met so far.

We walked into the hallway. We turned left, then right, right, left, straight, then finally left. In front of us stood the entrance to the classroom. The nameplate read *Ms. Zooka Room 3*. Mr. Mean opened the door and walked in. I could hear her excited voice as the teacher tried to engage the students.

"Now, George Washington was a great leader." Oh, George Washington. I had already learned about him. Ms. Zooka talked in a singsong voice. It was high and cheery. I peeked around the door frame. Mr. Mean cleared his throat, and Ms. Zooka looked at him.

"Oh! Mr. Mean! What do we owe the honor?" They did not see me, because I was still watching them from behind the door frame.

"Well," Mr. Mean said slowly, probably trying to raise the suspense. "You guys have a new classmate. Her name is…"

Ms. Zooka interrupted him.

"Oh goodie, a new student!!!" she said excitedly. Mr. Mean cleared his throat.

"As I was saying… We have a new student. Her name is Luna Moon." Mr. Mean poked his head out and gestured for me to come in.

Just as I was about to step in the room, someone called out "Moon Moon! What kind of name is that?" Some people snickered. Others laughed. I stepped in front of the class.

When they saw me, they all became quiet. My eyes swept the crowd. The only person talking was the girl… Summer, I think? She did not even look at me. Ms. Zooka finally spoke up.

"Well, you'll need someone to help you around. Summer, how about you?"

Summer jumped to attention at the sound of her name. When she saw me, her eyes nearly popped out of her head. And trust me, I know. I have seen a video about it. Do not ask.

"Come on, Summer," Ms. Zooka cajoled.

Summer slowly walked towards the front of the room, her eyes never leaving my face. Finally, she stood in front of me. Ms. Zooka introduced us. "Summer, this is Luna Moon, and Luna, this is Summer Vinely." Summer stuck out her right hand. I stuck out my left, copying her. Everyone laughed. Blushing, I took my hand back.

"Hi Luna! I'm Summer, official class clown and prankster. Hey, knock knock!" I stared at her blankly. "You're supposed to say 'Who's there?'" she whispered loud enough for the whole class to hear. *What was she going to do?*

"Who's there?" I asked cautiously. Summer smiled.

"Boo." The class groaned.

Someone called out, "Not this again!"

Another yelled, "Her jokes are terrible!" Summer winked at me.

"You're supposed to say 'boo who,'" she told me. *What was a joke?*

"Boo who?" I replied uncertainly. Summer's grin got even bigger.

"Don't cry, it's just a joke!" Summer and the class shouted together.

"Hey, you guys stole my punch line!" Summer hollered to the class, beaming. "Okay, I'll try again. Just DON'T mess it up," she said, shooting a warning glare to the class. "Why did the chicken cross the road?" Summer asked me.

"Why?" I asked, confused.

"To get to the other side!" Everyone except the teachers and I yelled. Summer rolled her eyes and sighed, but she looked happy, not annoyed. Summer started another one.

"Why did the chicken cross the play-"

"That's quite enough," said a grinning Ms. Zooka. "Luna, there is an empty seat next to Summer. Everything you need is in your desk." I sat down and saw who sat around me. Summer was to my left, Janice to my right, and a boy behind me with chocolate brown skin, black hair, and brown eyes so dark, it looked black and almost blended with the pupils. Those eyes look familiar…

"Well, back to what I was saying." Mr. Mean had left. "You're going to take your test on George Washington tomorrow. Class dismissed." A strange whistle went through the entire school. "Oh, and Luna? Can I talk to you?" I nodded. Everybody rushed out of the room as fast as they could. Everyone except Summer and I. I walked up to Ms. Zooka's desk. "Here is your schedule and locker combination. If you need help with either, ask Summer." Ms. Zooka handed me a piece of paper. "And, Luna? You don't have to take the test. I haven't taught it to you yet, so if you need me to help you…"

I shook my head.

"No, I think I know George Washington well enough. Thank you anyway."

"What classes do you have next?" Summer appeared behind me and snatched my schedule. "No way! You're in all my classes! And our lockers are next to each other! We have chemistry next." Summer made a face. "Every class we sit in the same spots, though. If you get a bad seat, it's a bummer; otherwise it's okay. Lunch is after art. Got it?" I nodded. I understood. Sort of. Summer and I grabbed our things and walked out.

What still puzzled me was the concept of a locker. What was a locker? And why did you need a combination? I took back my paper from her, and saw my locker number. *Locker 17, A4, Combo: 24, 15, 10.* We reached our lockers. "Have you ever had a locker before?" Summer asked as she saw me struggling with mine, as soon as I found it. My locker was gray and had a strange lock on it.

"Nooooo," I said hesitantly. Her grin never left her face.

"Awesome! I love teaching people how to use them!" She seemed excited. "You store your things in it so you don't have to lug your books everywhere. Okay. So, you see this lock?" She pointed to the strange lock.

"Yes…" I said uncertainly.

"Okay, then you turn this knob to the numbers that it goes to. So, your locker combo is 24, 15, 10, right? So then, you turn the knob to the right to 24, then to the left to 15, and then to the right again to 10. Simple. Got it?"

I nodded, then started working on the lock. About two seconds later, the locker was open.

"WOW. I think you broke the record for the fastest locker opening," Summer said, staring at me, wide eyed. What? Cool? Awesome? Wow?

"Um… Summer?" She was closing her locker. She had put her things away.

"Yeah?" she answered absentmindedly.

My words burst out. "What do things mean? Cool? Awesome? Wow? What do they *mean*?" I stuffed my things inside my locker, then closed the door.

"Um… how do I explain?" Summer laughed nervously. "O-okay. So, you know how everyone uses great, amazing, etcetera? Well, some kid, we don't know who, made up some words to mean that, but with some pizazz."

"Pizazz?" I was still kind of confused. Summer sighed.

"Jazzy, extra flair, awesomer, better than better. Anything else?" Summer looked at the clock. "Come on, we're going to be late!" She started walking fast towards the classroom, pulling me behind her.

"Who is our next teacher?"

"Lucas, the boy who sat behind you,'s dad. Mr. Wallstone. Lucas is awesome at chemistry, like his dad. Lucas can whip up something that will knock you out cold, no prob." We walked into the chemistry lab.

"So this is the famous Miss Moon I've heard all about." Mr. Wallstone looked just like his son. He had nut brown skin, raven hair, and dark tree bark eyes. He was wearing dark blue pants and a black shirt.

"Yes, Sir," I replied.

"Hum... I wonder... Do you like chemistry?" Mr. Wallstone asked pleasantly.

"From what I have done so far, yes." Which was nothing. I only liked it because of what I saw. And what I saw was chemicals blowing up in that one kids' face. It was hilarious. Mr. Wallstone looked at a piece of paper on his desk.

"Well, since Summer is your student helper, we'll pair you up with her. Maddie, you'll be with Lucas." Maddie, the girl I saw hand-slapping Summer earlier, shot me a dark look. Maddie had vibrant red hair and crystal blue eyes, and right now, those eyes promised death for me.

Mr. Wallstone asked us to mix chemicals until we found a mixture that would make someone feel sad for no apparent reason. We set to work with our partners. As Summer and I were blending the chemicals together, I asked another question.

"Um, Summer, what is a joke?" I whispered. She nearly dropped her vial.

"You don't know what a joke is?" She seemed shocked. I half expected her to start screaming at me like Mr. Shrude. "WHAT KIND OF FREAK DOESN'T KNOW WHAT A JOKE IS?" I imagined her yelling. Instead, Summer just sighed.

"A joke is a funny comment." A wicked grin crossed her face. "Like why did the chicken cross the playground?" *What is a playground? I will just pretend I know. Besides, I know this question or, as she put it, joke. She said it earlier.*

"To get to the other side," I answered confidently.

"No," Summer said, choking with laughter. "To get to the other SLIDE!" she howled. Everyone froze and looked at us. My face suddenly warmed up, and I slouched in my seat, trying to be invisible. It's really hard though, when your partner is howling with laughter and calling your name.

"Wasn't that a good one Luna? Huh? Huh?" The only one not looking at us was Lucas. He was staring intensely at his work, a stack of books beside him.

"I got it!" he suddenly shouted, standing up. The chemicals in his vial were a dark, murky blue color. Lucas accidentally spilled a little on himself, and his smile turned into a frown. "Why is everyone so happy?" he said, tears spilling down his cheeks. "Here you go, dad," Lucas said, hiccuping. "The effects wear off in a few minutes."

Mr. Wallstone started clapping.

"Well done Lucas. Well done." By the time Mr. Wallstone had finished speaking, the whole class was clapping.

"I guess I get an A then," said a smug Maddie, but no one noticed her.

CHAPTER 8

"That's called an applause," Summer explained while we jammed our books into our lockers. "Come on, it's P.E. and then Art. We're almost there."

I was excited. I loved this way of learning. How did Summer put it? With *friends*. Even though I already knew these subjects really well, I could just *chat*.

We walked into a changing room. Summer said that is where we change clothes. *Why would I change my clothes when I already have good ones on?* I asked Summer.

"Well," Summer replied, her hand on her hip. "The school asks you to do it. If you don't want to get in trouble, then you do it, but since you don't have a uniform..." Summer slipped into a stall and locked it. "Then I guess you can wear what you're wearing."

I shrugged.

"Okay! See you out there," I told her. We were the only people left in the changing room.

When I finally found my way to the gym, everyone was wearing the same thing. They were wearing a white short-sleeved shirt with white shorts. The sides of the shorts had two stripes on them, one green and one blue. A huge person started walking towards me. Summer said the P.E. teacher was a bodybuilder. The man had dirt colored hair and onyx eyes. He was wearing a yellow short-sleeved shirt and black shorts. I could also see a whistle glistening on his shirt.

"Hiya Luna," the man said gruffly, with a huge smile and twinkling eyes. He had a strange accent. "Today we're gonna play dodgeball. You any good at that? Or at least know how to play?"

"You… dodge a ball?" That was what the name implied, anyway. I hoped I was right.

"Well, kinda," he said, chuckling. "Ho! I forgot! My name is Mr. Elk. Anyway, there are two teams. The balls are in the middle, there." Mr. Elk pointed to the middle of the rectangular room. "You're trying not to get hit or to hit your team-mates with a ball. If you get hit, then you sit next to my desk, cuz youuuu'reee out!" He pounded his desk with a loud *THA-THUMP!* "At the same time, you're trying to hit the people on the other team." Then, calling to the whole class, he shouted, "Same teams! Luna's on Team A!"

Team A cheered. I looked at my teammates. Lucas was on my team. I didn't recognize anyone else, though. Summer and Janice were on Team B.

"Just so you know," Summer whispered to me over the front lines, "I'm very competitive. You mess with my team, you mess with me." A devilish smile creeped on her face.

"You're going down Luna," Janice whispered, no sign of amusement on her face.

"Ready!" Mr. Elk called. "Set! GOOO!!" *Tweeeeet! Tweet, tweet, tweet!* Everyone made a grab for the balls, but they were not there. I guess it was okay to use my "super speed" (compared to them) for a minute. Five balls, five shots. Ten people on each team. NO misses. I calculated the outcomes. I hit out five people.

The only people quick enough to get out of the way were Summer, Maddie, a very skinny boy, a girl who did a ton of turns and flips, and a straw haired guy. Summer's team, with the balls I threw at them, hit out five of my teammates. I gathered up the balls, and hit out everyone *except* Summer and Maddie on the other team. Then they pummeled the rest of my team. The people started chanting.

"Luna! Luna! Luna!" They were chanting for... me?

I had two balls, they had three. I shot one with deadly accuracy, and hit Summer. "Good game!" she called over all of the clamor. Summer joined in all of the shouting.

"Luna! Luna!" The cheering got louder. One ball left.

Maddie looked furious. She desperately shot all four of her balls, and not one found its mark. I was too fast. *After all, no one can kill me.* Wait, what did I just think? *I should hurt her.* What is going on? These thoughts were not mine. I aimed for her stomach, and restrained myself from throwing hard enough to destroy her. After I checked that she was okay, I told Mr. Elk I needed to go to the bathroom, then ran off.

Soon after jogging the hallways for a minute, I heard someone call out "Luna! Wait up!" I considered speeding up. "You don't even know where the bathroom is," she said, seeing me debate myself. I sighed, and let Summer catch up.

"Where is the bathroom?" I asked in one breath.

"The one next to the Art room? You just missed it. Listen, Luna, I know when someone really doesn't need to go to the bathroom. I've used that trick my whole life. What is going on? I can help, you know."

No, she could not. I wanted to tell her everything right now, to tell her I was a fugitive on the run, an orphan, a freak. To tell her everything, but I could not. Unless I wanted to lose my only (and first) true friend. Unless I wanted to blow my cover. Unless I wanted to get exposed and captured again. I could not.

"I-I cannot tell," I stammered nervously.

"Okay, fine." Summer sighed. She pulled something out of her pocket. "Here. Have a piece of chocolate. Chocolate makes everything better."

I put the little brown square in my mouth. Its smooth, rich taste exploded on my tongue.

"Oh my goodness, this is amazing! Where did you get it?" I asked. Maybe I could get some for myself later!

Summer shrugged.

"My parents own the town chocolate shop. Nothing much," she said offhandedly. *THE Chocolate Shop? MY chocolate shop?* I definitely was interested.

"I love chocolate!" I exclaimed. She shrugged again.

"It's an official fact that every human being loves chocolate," she said, smiling slightly. That was when it clicked. H-B. Human Being. Summer smiled slyly. "Hey, maybe you could come over tonight?" *Tonight?* I jumped out of my shock induced daze from my realization.

"I-I should probably talk to my parents first," I replied.

"Yeah, I guess that's a good idea," Summer said, sounding disappointed. "Come on, we are going to be late."

CHAPTER 9

We started running down the hall towards the Art classroom. I thought about PE again, and how I had that weird urge to hurt Maddie. I had to have better control over my thoughts. *I mean, who thinks such thoughts? What messed up person wants to hurt people?* That kind of thinking is evil. *Okay, control, complete control. Let's do this.* I walked into the Art classroom.

"So great you could join us ladies. My name is Mr. Mongar." A cold, tingling feeling crept up my spine. Mr. Mongar had coal black hair, in a haircut I saw once in a picture of men in green suits with the word *Navy* on it. He had beetle black eyes, and he was wearing a jumpsuit with patches of green and brown. Mr. Mongar also had shiny brown work boots. His voice was a steel post.

"You'll be sitting next to Summer, as you probably guessed. Right in the front, where the trouble-makers are." The teacher gave a cold, cruel smile, almost identical to Mr. Shrude's. He could not be Mr. Shrude though. Could he?

I sat next to Summer. The tables only had two people at each. Mr. Mongar walked up towards the chalkboard. "Today, we are going to be drawing... vampires." *What are vampires?* "Yes," Mr. Mongar said, soaking up the silent excitement from the rest of the classroom. "Vampires. The *supposedly* mythical people who drink blood and are only active at night. Why, you may ask? Because daylight burns their skin, eventually killing them." *Ew. Blood is disgusting. Just imagining having to <u>drink</u> it made me want to throw up.*

"Now, you all know about vampires. Well, I'm going to show you how to draw one." Mr. Mongar started drawing a scary, dark, bat-like creature with long fangs. When he finished the draft, Mr. Mongar passed out paper and pencils. Summer whispered to me out of the corner of her mouth.

"Mr. Mongar is someone you don't want to get caught by." Summer took a straw out of her bag and ripped a corner off a piece of paper. She rolled the paper up and placed it in the straw. She closed one eye, aiming the straw at the ceiling above Mr. Mongar's desk. Mr. Mongar sat down at his desk. Summer blew on the straw, hard, the little piece of paper shooting out and hitting the ceiling tile above his head. Suddenly, it started raining feathers on him. I stared at Summer, horrified. "I said caught," she said, winking. "Now go back to work or he'll suspec-"

"Vinely! Detention!" Mr. Mongar roared. Summer tried to put on an innocent face.

"Whatever for? That?" Summer pointed towards the feather mess. "I didn't do that!" Summer said, seeming offended. "I was drawing, like you said to!" Summer held up her drawing. Next to her draft, Mr. Mongar's looked like a tangle of lines. Summer's drawing was almost life-like, almost as if it could leap out of the page. Summer was, without a doubt, finished.

I looked at my own drawing. I did not copy the board, like Summer, I had just sketched from the head to the waist. It was a woman. The woman looked familiar... melted eyes, a soft smile... Then it hit me. The woman is Eva! I had drawn Eva!

"And what have you drawn, Moon?" Mr. Mongar snarled, angry at being foiled. I did not like his tone, probably because it sounded so much like Mr. Shrude. It was uncanny, how much they were alike. Before I could lift my paper, he snached it from my grip.

"I said vampires, not people!" Mr. Mongar growled like an enraged grizzly bear. "Next strike Moon, and you'll get detention too."

Art class just got worse. I got a new sheet of paper and tried to copy what Mr. Mongar had drawn, but it's hard to concentrate when he was looking over my shoulder constantly. Mr. Mongar checked all of the tables, but he seemed to prefer ours. Once, he went to Janice's table. Then, surprise! Mr. Mongar came back to me and Summer. Mr. Mongar checked on Lucas, who was secretly reading a book under the table, but pretended to work until Mr. Mongar left his area before continuing to read. Mr. Mongar, after leaving Lucas, drifted to our desk. Finally, everyone finished up the detail they were working on, and the long hour was over.

CHAPTER 10

Summer and I started walking towards the cafeteria. Well, I was more like following Summer. "What is detention?" I asked her.

"A really mean thing teachers do. I mean, they make you stay after school!" Summer turned towards me, her face twisted into an expression of dismay. Stay after school? Sounds great! No, not great, more like... awesoomie!

"Wow, you are so lucky. Did I use wow right?" I asked quickly afterward. Summer stared at me like I had said Mr. Mongar was the nicest person in the world.

"Yeah, you used wow right, but lucky? Are you crazy! Mr. Mongar is the teacher that watches the students in detention! Besides, you don't do anything! You just sit there and stare at the wall," Summer exclaimed as we opened the doors and stepped inside the huge cafeteria.

Tables and chairs are everywhere, and so were students. There were few empty tables. Each table was crammed with students of every kind of shape, size, and color. There are also huge windows, but what really caught my eye was the long line of kids. I followed the lines with my eyes to see two doors, about two yards apart, students streaming in with nothing, then spilling out with a tray and... was that food? Summer led me to the back of the line. When we were at the back of the line, she pulled out three green rectangles. The rectangles had a one in each corner. Dollars.

"This is money. If you don't know what this is," Summer said, wagging the bills in my face.

"I know what money is," I said, annoyed. I shouldn't be annoyed though. Summer should be. She kept explaining what I needed to know, and what seems to be common knowledge here. Soon, we were at the front of the line.

"It was a joke. Just grab what you want," Summer mumbled as we came through the door. I grabbed a tray off a rack, like Summer. I had to choose a drink next. The choices were milk, chocolate milk, or juice. Normally, I would have choosen chocolate milk, but because of recent events, I didn't really trust that choice anymore. So, I chose juice instead. Next was what the sign said was fruits and vegetables. I chose a yellow curved one. The sign said it was a banana. After that, it was hot dogs or pizza. I chose a hot dog. I slid down the line. The person at the cash register was a lady. She wore a hairnet and a black apron.

"How are you paying?" she droned in a well rehearsed voice.

"Put it on the Moon tab?" I answered, doing what Eva told me to do if I ever needed to pay for something.

"The ones who work for the government?" the lady asked. I nodded. "Okay, put it on the government's tab, you're free," she said, after clicking around on the register. I followed Summer and walked out the second door. I quickened my steps until Summer was beside me.

"Hey, I'm going to sit with Maddie today, okay?" Summer asked.

"Okay. See you later." Did I do that right? I made my way over to one of the rare empty tables. I sat down, putting my tray on the counter. As I was looking at the banana, trying to figure out how to eat it, I saw movement out of the corner of my eyes. I looked up from my stubborn banana. People were snagging their trays and standing up from their table. Some ran, some walked, but they all made their way over to me. Soon I was swarmed by a cloud of students at a used-to-be empty table. People started calling my name.

"Hey, Luna, sorry for making fun of your name. I'm Ryan." As soon as he stopped talking, another voice popped out of the midst.

"Luna! My name is Hannah!" Then another.

"I'm Maria." And another.

"John."

"Priya!"

"Lucy."

"Marco!"

"Dominique."

"Carmen!"

"Emily!"

Finally, the loudest voice of them all rang out. It was Janice. "Guys, be quiet! She's had a long day and she can't meet *everyone*!" I smiled gratefully. I felt like everyone, even the people whose classes I was not in, had come to see me.

A teeny girl in front of me held up an iPad, not unlike the ones I saw Mr. Shrude use. The girl had amber pigtails and bronze eyes. She reminded me of Summer. "Look, you've already gotten a million likes on Youtube!" the girl exclaimed, showing me the iPad.

A video played on the screen. It was the gym, with dodgeballs flying. The screen turned. A pale girl, with ashy blonde hair moving at my regular speed, throwing dodgeballs... me. Oh no. So much for not attracting attention. In the corner of the screen, I saw the title of the video. *INCREDI*BALL*!!!!!!* They all stared in amazement as I nailed Summer. Maddie threw her balls. Suddenly, for a second, you could see a creepy smile made of pure evil fill my face. Then, as quickly as it had appeared, it disappeared, and I slammed the ball into Maddie's stomach. Then the video stopped.

"Pretty great, right? I'm Anna," the teeny girl with the tablet said, smiling at me and bouncing on her toes. I nodded, even though my gut twisted. I was exposed! On a website! I had no idea what a website was, but now anyone could see me. I was exposed. To everyone.

I finally figured out how to open my banana. I ate the inside. It was good. No, better than good, it was awesoomie. Better than drinking chocolate milk every day. No, night. I am very confused. *Was it getting hotter in here?* I looked around. The windows were nowhere near me. I started shivering. It was suddenly very cold. Then hot. *Was I sick?* I had never been sick before, I had only heard of it. I just wanted to lay down. The chatter around me stopped. Everyone started staring at me. I did not care. My mind was foggy, like a thick mist had settled over it. It was hard to think. *Wait... who am I? What are these people doing?* I shook my head. *I am Luna V. Moon. Escapee from... Mr. Shrude. I have a... friend, named... Summer. I can see, hear, and smell for ten miles.* The fog fought back. I was losing to myself. My eyelids became heavy. My face felt thicker and pins and needles pricked and poked at it. *I will not close my eyes.*

"Luna, are you okay?" someone asked, sounding a million universes away. *I will not close my eyes.* People were moving around, but I could not concentrate. I could not hear. I could not see. I could not move. I could not do anything. My body was on fire. Then dumped in dry ice.

"Here Luna, have some chocolate," someone said slowly, like they were talking underwater. Chocolate? I opened my eyes as wide as I could, which was not very big. Maybe halfway?

"Now isn't the best time for chocolate, Luna needs to go to the hospital!!" a hysteric someone else shouted. In slow motion, I reached for the chocolate... and put it in my mouth. By the time it was in my mouth, they realized I had taken the candy.

"NO!" they all screamed as I swallowed. Instantly, the fog cleared. The needles and pins disappeared. My face did not seem so big. My eyelids popped open. I could see, hear, and smell again. I had all of the energy in the world. I was not hot, nor cold, but just right. I looked at my food. I was definitely not going to eat anymore. I searched through my memory. Did Summer say anything about what was after lunch? No.

"Hey guys, I am going to the nurse, I do not feel so well," I told everyone, wanting to get away from the mass of students. Janice shoved herself forward.

"Good idea. I'll take you. Come on," Janice offered. I stood up as she finally stood beside me. As we got started walking towards the door, the crowd parted for us, so we could get through to the doors. We strode through them.

As we started walking down the hall I zoned out, and let Janice guide me. *Why was I suddenly sick? And why did chocolate make me feel better?* As usual, millions of questions, but no answers.

"Hey Luna! Luna! LuNA!" Janice pulled me from my trance. "We're here. Hope you feel better," she said. I waved at her.

"Good-bye," I told her as Janice started walking towards the cafeteria. I went into the nurse's office.

CHAPTER 11

The nurse was fat. There was no other way to say it. She took up four folding chairs just to sit down. Her desk, just so she could fit, took up one-fourth of the room. Half of the room had 'beds' and curtains that could be pulled around each individual for privacy. The rest of the room had a sink and cabinets full of medical supplies. The nurse was sleeping. I could tell by her thunder-like snores. This was the first time I had actually seen a real person sleep, but from my study, she was definitely sleeping.

"Excuse me? Mrs. Nurse?" I whispered. She snorted and flopped her head to her other shoulder, with such force that her tongue leaped out of her mouth. "Excuse me, Mrs. Nurse?" I asked louder, taking a few more steps closer to the desk, which was at the far corner of the room. "Mrs. Nurse?" I half shouted. She did not wake up. "EXCUSE ME!" I yelled. The nurse snorted again as she woke up.

"What? What is it?" she asked blearily. She had short black hair and baseball sized glasses for her baseball sized eyes. Her eyes were as dark as her hair; dark as the darkest day. *Or was it night?* I was more confused than ever. *Would I face more nice people or mean people? What was I? Who did I belong with?* The nurse was fully awake now. "Oh, new student. My name is Nurse Vortex. What you need?" Nurse Vortex asked, sounding bored.

"I-I do not feel well," I stuttered. This overweight nurse was making me uncomfortable. Nurse Vortex sighed. With difficulty, she got out of her chairs, and lumbered over to me, grabbing things from the nearby supply cabinet. Then she started checking me here and there, with grace I did not know she had. Eventually, Nurse Vortex said she had one more thing to do.

"I'm going to check your pulse. Stick out your hand," she ordered, and obediently, I did. "Hummm…" she whispered, looking thoughtful. "Faint pulse," Nurse Vortex said, wondering. "Faint pulse? FAINT PULSE!" She almost screamed as realization crossed her face. "WE GOT TO GET YOU TO THE HOSPITAL!" she shrieked urgently. "WE GOT TO GET YOU AN AMBULANCE!" Nurse Vortex practically dived for the phone on her desk.

"I-I am fine!" I said, shocked, my hands up.
"Really!" Nurse Vortex was gasping from the effort.
"You'll feel fine one minute-" *gasp* "-and pass
out the next. I-" *gasp* "-know it!" She was now wres-
tling the pile of clutter for her phone, trying not to
let it fall. I turned and sprinted like Summer and
Janice, down the hall. It was not really sprinting
for me, more like jogging, but I had to blend in.

"Hey!" *gasp* "Come ba-" *gasp* "-ck here!" choked
the nurse. *FWOOMP!* I am guessing that was her
tower of junk as it fell. *Tomb-pa. Tomb-pa.* Nurse
Vortex was coming. I ran past some bathrooms.
ToMb-pa. ToMb-Pa. She was getting closer.

*"Can we please go a little faster? I mean, we can
beat her!" complained my Lazy side.*

*"No!" My Logic side ordered. "We may be able
to beat her, but that would mean exposing us even
MORE!"*

*"Come on!" My Lazy side pleaded. "Who would
believe that oversized nurse?"*

*"MR. SHRUDE, THAT'S WHO!" Stormed
Logic. "I can not belive you!" Logic muttered.*

"Be quiet you two," I said in my head.

TOMB-PA! TOMB-PA! I had stopped running.
The bathrooms were a foot back.

"Co-" *gasp* "-me ba-" *gasp* "-ck he-" *gasp* "-re!"
The nurse heaved, *tomb-pa-*ing her way over. How

could I escape? I could not keep running, I did not know this place. Well, I knew a few things, but not that much.

Wait. The bathrooms. I ran (as I would) over to the bathroom door and slipped inside. One stall had an out-of-order sign taped on it, but I did not pay any notice. I looked around, trying to find a window. There were none.

"When I do not need a window, there are tons, but when I do, there is not even one!" I mumbled, fuming quietly. Wait. An "Out-of-Order" sign. As I started tinkering with a plan, I realized something. I am an escape artist. I was not an escapee anymore. Only a real escape artist would have snuck away from the only place I had ever known, and go into a strange building. Suddenly, I had an idea.

The "Out-of-Order" stall! No one goes in there. If I can go in there, punch a hole in the corner, and slip through, then I am home free! Sort of. Sooooo, I went into the out-of-order stall. I found the corner. Two inches from the corner, I punched a hole. It was not big, and it had small poles of black metal on the edges. The bathroom door opened.

"I know you're-" *grunt* "-in there. You can't-" *grunt* "-hide forever!" *grunt. She is here! I got to go!* I started crawling through the hole I made, getting scratched by the metal. Eventually, I wiggled through, getting as much as my torso out, when *it* started. The burning. I kept squirming, almost screaming in agony.

"I know you're in there." *Creak, SLAM.* "You can't hide forever." *Creak, SLAM.* She's checking the stalls! *Creak, SLAM.* Only two more stalls before she would reach mine! Faster, *faster! Creak, SLAM.* I had not made the hole big enough. My arms were still stuck on the other side of the wall. *Creak. SLAM.* She was going to find me!

CHAPTER 12

"Aw, man, why did I close the doors?" Nurse Vortex moaned to herself. "Now I have to recheck them all!" *Creak, shuffle. Creak.*

I had to move! Aha! Only the tips of my fingers were trapped against my legs now. *Creak.* Free! I looked around for something to help pull my legs out. I grabbed the grass and yanked. I had now had pain beyond what I had ever experienced. My arms felt like they were getting ripped from their sockets, and my legs were getting scratched to ribbons. Plus, I felt like I was disintegrating, bit by bit. I kept pulling, kept climbing. I gritted my teeth.

"Come on. Come on!" I mumbled through my grating teeth. I could hear kids behind the bushes in front of me.

"Get it, get it! Ooohhh, Lisa, you're the monkey!" a voice called out.

"Sarah, throw the frisbee here!"

"Man, why didn't you catch it?" someone sighed. "Fine, I'll get it." A yellow disk suddenly flew towards me and landed *inches* away. Footsteps came towards me. Someone passed through the bushes. "Luna, what are you doing here!" Summer exclaimed. As she looked at the situation I was in, she broke into a wide grin. "I never knew there was a hole here. Who are you running away from? I won't tell," Summer whispered as she picked up the yellow disk. I did not want to tell her. "Vortex? Zooka? Mongar? *Who?*" I gulped.

"Nurse Vortex," I said in a small voice.

"I run away from her all of the time. Once, I put shaving cream in her hand, and tickled her face with a feather. Vortex smeared the shaving cream *all over* her face. When she woke up, guess what? She *ate* it! Vortex was soooo mad!" Summer laughed at the memory, then sighed. "The only reason I'm playing this game is because I was going to the boys bathroom to superglue the lids shut, when my sister, Anna, came up to me and asked me to play. Anna said she would tell on me if she ever saw me setting up a prank again." I cleared my throat. "Oh, right, sorry." Summer grabbed my arms and tried to heave me out. A couple of centimeters down, a lot more to go. "You're really stuck, aren't ya?" she grunted. "Okay, one, two, three, HEAVE!" Summer yanked.

"Last oonee." Nurse Vortex's voice shot out like a bullet.

"You didn't tell me she was still chasing you!" Summer whispered, eyes wide with fear.

"Hurry up!" I whispered urgently.

"I'm trying!" Summer quietly exclaimed. I wanted to scream in frustration and agony.

"Summer, stop playing weak and punch the wall already!" I exclaimed. Summer dropped my arms in surprise.

"P-punch the wall?" she stuttered.

"Yes! Punch the wall!" I squawked. Summer punched.

"Owwww!" she proclaimed, cradling her hand. Her punch did nothing. I sighed.

"Summer, promise you will not tell anybody," I said desperately.

"Tell what?" she asked.

"Promise!" I pleaded.

"Okay, I promise, I promise!" Summer said hurriedly. I bashed some of the wall, and it crumbled away easily. I slipped out. Summer stared, open mouthed. "What... How..."

"RUN!" I yelled. Summer ran. I jogged (for me. I looked like I was running to Summer). Soon, we stopped. We were both panting. I was gasping from the heat, although I do not know about Summer.

"I can't... run... anymore." Summer fought for breath, her hands on her knees. I was about to say I could run all night if it was not for this heat, but decided against it. Summer was not faking it. I truly was different. My hope was to find someone else like me, but now that hope went down the drain. Summer stood up straight. "So why were you running away from Vortex?" Summer had asked the one question I did not want her to answer.

"Uhhh..." How was I supposed to explain that Nurse Vortex wanted to take me to the hospital (whatever that is) because I had a faint pulse? That I was different from everyone else, and that I was sweating more water than the ocean? I would explain it the simple way... by not explaining it at all.

"Is there a fan nearby?" I asked Summer to take her attention away from Nurse Vortex.

"No. It's *Fall*. It's *cold* out here," she answered, a confused expression on her face. I actually think she was cold. Summer was wearing a jacket and was still shivering a bit. Okay, so it was just me on the really hot thing too.

"Let's go inside," Summer said, gesturing to a nearby door. We stepped inside. Summer stopped shuddering and I was not burning to death. "So," Summer said, hands on her hips. "Spill." I searched my brain, grasping an idea, any idea.

"I... asked for... some... headache medicine," I blurted out. "Then... she *insisted* on fully inspecting me. And, uh, I refused, and ran away." Summer sighed at my explanation.

"Fine, you won't tell me? Okay I respect your privacy, but... why won't you tell me?" she asked, waiting for an answer.

"It is complicated, okay!" I said, exasperated. "I do not think anyone would understand," I whispered.

"Fine, won't ask. Just, promise you'll come to my birthday sleepover tomorrow. Please?" Summer pleaded.

"Okay, I promise." I replied. It is the least I could do, seeing she was keeping my strength a secret. So far.

"Well, come on, we're going to be late for math with Ms. Marlock, 'The Vulture.' "

CHAPTER 13

We slid into our seats as the bell rang. "Do the problem on the board," Ms. Marlock croaked. "When you're done, come to me and I'll check it."

Ms. Marlock looked withered. She had scraggly, uneven, greasy ink-black hair. Her pursed mouth pushed out farther than a mouth should go, making it look like a small beak. Ms. Marlock had beady black eyes, and seemed to squint all of the time. She was wearing a plain wine red dress, with similar colored shoes.

Speaking of shoes, my feet were aching. Why would anyone wear shoes? It is a waste of time, and makes you want to chop your feet off. I took out a piece of paper and a pencil. Pencils are *much* better than pens. You can erase your mistakes! *How cool-awesome-good? Oh, whatever it is!* The problem on the board said:

$$5x + 3 = 6x + 2$$
What is x?

I solved it right away. It was one of the easiest things I had ever done in my life. The answer, obviously, was x = 1. I brought it up to the teacher's desk where Ms. Marlock was gazing at the other students, enjoying their difficulty with the problem. When she saw me, her insane grin turned into a fierce frown. I silently handed her my paper. She took a sticky note from a drawer in her desk. Ms. Marlock looked at my work, then the sticky note. Then my work. Then the sticky note. She kept doing this, going faster and faster, her mouth opening wider and wider, her squinty eyes actually bulging. Ms. Marlock finally looked at me. "How… What…" she stuttered. "Where is your work?" she eventually spit out.

"I did it in my head," I said simply, shrugging.

"Wha… that's preposterous! What is five hundred times four divided by nine?" As soon as Ms. Marlock finished, I answered her.

"Two hundred twenty two and two tenths repeated."

"One thousand times eight to the seventh power?"

"Two billion ninety-seven million one hundred fifty-two thousand."

"Eighty-six thousand two hundred fifty-four times three divided by six?"

"Forty-three thousand one hundred twenty-seven." *Wow, these are really easy questions.* Ms. Marlock sighed after she checked the answers on a calculator.

"I believe you. No one could or would memorize such random math problems. Since everyone will most likely spend the rest of class working on this problem that they will never solve without help, you can read, work on other homework, or something else," she told me.

The rest of the period I spent drawing pictures of Eva, Ivy, or some of the landscapes I saw by moonlight on the rooftops before I ran away. After dumping her work (yes, Summer *actually* dumped her work) on Ms. Marlock's desk, Summer came to "help" me clean up my twenty or so papers (the periods were over an hour long) after the strange whistle blew through the school (skol?). As she came over, I hurriedly gathered my papers in a not-so-neat stack.

"Ugh, that problem was *so* hard," Summer complained as she waited for me. Summer snatched a picture from my pile. Before she could look at it, I grabbed a side. I tugged at it, intending for her to let go. Summer pulled the paper. I yanked. She heaved again. I felt the paper ripping, so I let go.

The sketch probably was not important. "Who's this?" Summer asked curiously. I looked at her.

"Who?"

She handed me the paper.

"Her." Those colorless eyes were already melted, staring at me. She was smiling.

"My… caretaker," I said cautiously.

"What's her name?" Summer asked, tearing her eyes from the picture and looking at me.

"Um…"

"What's that?" Summer was looking at the landscape at the top of the stack. It was a view of The Chocolate Shop. From that roof you could see The Chocolate Shop perfectly and the smell…

"A place." I put the drawing of Eva on top of the landscape. Summer shrugged and turned away.

"It looks like my parents' chocolate shop." Summer turned suddenly. "Is it?" Ms. Marlock, who I had not even known was still there, saved me.

"Get out of my classroom," Ms. Marlock whispered. I hurriedly grabbed my papers and left.

✰✰✰

I ran (not like Summer) to my little corner, then dashed back to the school yard. I watched what people did, staying in the shadows so I would not get too hot. It was chilly, there in the shadows. That is probably what Summer felt before. In the sunlight, Maddie touched Janice.

"Tag!" Maddie shouted. "You're it!" she yelled, racing away from Janice. Janice, looking around for a victim, saw me.

"Hey, want to play?" she asked.

"No, I am fine," I replied, sinking into the shade. I pressed against the wall, watching the game and thinking. *A sleepover with Summer? Okay, you seriously sleep over at the person's house, but that is _all_ you do?*

Soon, all of the kids got their lumpty-strappy-things and started walking to their homes. *What I was going to do in the meantime while I waited for school tomorrow?* I had no idea. Maybe take a quick peek around the orpha... er... whatever it was called, because it was not an orphanage. I needed to do one thing before I went over there. I sprinted (not like Summer) to my little alley and took my socks and shoes off. What a relief! I stretched my toes, then took off. I zipped around, twirling, jumping, and leaping. I was free! -Ish. Then I saw the people. I forgot that people come out. I hope all they saw was a blur. I ran faster, trying to find someplace empty.

☆ ☆ ☆

Finally, I did. Near *The* Building. You know, I think I am going to call it that. From the outside, it looked like a run-down building. I wonder how I had never noticed that before. I slowed my pace, and kept myself in the shadows of the dark gloom. I could hear talking.

"Tonight you should test Its strength of mind and strategy. If Luna's going to be perfect, It's going to need strategy and strength of mind. But not too much. We don't want It thinking for Itself," a husky voice growled.

"Yes, Sir!" a too familiar voice replied. "And we'll catch and throw I-V in prison 567A if It shows any sign of Itself," added Mr. Shude, the too familiar voice. Woah. Luna was me! And maybe I-V was Ivy? That is why they were testing me. To get my incrediball "powers" to grow, to grow under *their* control. If I got out of hand, I would be controlled again. A red light glowed all around me. Sunset.

"I will be back. Same time tomorrow," the new voice said authoritatively. A door opened and closed. Then Mr. Shrude sighed, from what I could hear. I heard him walking. Back and forth, back and forth.

"How to do it, how to do it," he muttered as he paced. After a while he said "Aha!"

A blood curdling shriek filled the air. I jumped, startled. Mr. Shrude started as well, surprised. His eyebrows creased. The shriek turned to crying, then sobbing. The person wailed in misery.

"She's gone!" the woman bawled. "Gone! All gone!" The person broke out into even greater, heavier, sobs. Eva! Mr. Shrude flung open the door and ran as fast as he could to Eva. *Like the kids at school, I am guessing. Or could he be like me?* Mr. Shrude shouted orders.

"Get in contact with the Commander! Ask him to get a search party for the entire Shenandoah Valley! Hurry! We got to get her before she goes far!" Mr. Shrude yelled. I could hear shouts all over the place after that.

I sprinted as fast as my legs could carry me away, *AWAY* from that Building and those cruel people. Away. but not farther than the edge of town. I could not leave. This was my home, whether I liked it or not.

☆☆☆

I sat down and stared at the empty woods surrounding the town. I could hear the sounds of rushing water and the rustle of the wind in the branches of the trees. My tense body finally relaxed. I felt calm. Well, as calmer than I was a few minutes ago.

I stayed there until dawn, hiding in the woods. When the first sun rays showered over the trees, I flew to my spot in the alley, avoiding the main roads. Mostly going through backyards. I finally got to my alley. I seized my things, making sure I grabbed my other pair of clothes, and unfortunately, my shoes, and sneaked into the schoolyard.

CHAPTER 14

I was tugging on my left and last shoe when Summer found me. The shoe finally slipped on.

"What did your mom say?" she asked, hands on her hips.

"She said yes!" I said, trying to sound cheerful.

"Yes!" Summer squealed. "After school we'll go straight to my house." The warning bell rang. We walked to Mrs. Zooka's room. We sat down as soon as Mrs. Zooka started talking.

"Roll call!" Mrs. Zooka twittered happily. "Dominque Lagos?"

"Here!" someone piped.

"John Marketa?" Mrs. Zooka called.

"Here," another boredly replied.

"Luna Moon?"

"Here!" I answered.

"Janice Doro?"

"Present."

"Summer Vinely?"

"Cheeseburger!" Snickers and giggles ran through the class at Summer's answer. Mrs. Zooka couldn't even keep from chuckling.

"Always a classic," the teacher muttered. Then Mrs. Zooka finished the roll call.

☆☆☆

"Okay class, tomorrow we are going to learn about one of the most crucial battles on Earth. Yes, I am talking about the Battle of Yorktown and the end of the Revolutionary War." Mrs. Zooka waited a while, probably for suspense. Of course, I already knew that topic. Eva had taught me every-thing about every battle in history. Mrs. Zooka started again. "But TODAY is the time for the test on George Washington! I hope you studied!" Groans crashed throughout the entire room. Mrs. Zooka walked around, handing out little packets.

I started trembling. *They did tests too?* I slouched in my seat, praying, *hoping*, that she would not see me. *They will probably do the Disaster-Master. And when I am in there, what will they do to me? Dunk me in an ice-cold water filled tank and leave me there for the rest of the day? Make me breathe in toxic gas? Scrape me with a million needles until I am half dead?* The thin packet slapped my desk. Summer wrote something on her paper, then whispered to me.

"What are you whimpering about? I mean, I know tests are hard, but they aren't *that* bad." Summer started writing on the paper again.

"Take your time and do your best. Answer the questions on your test!" Mrs. Zooka chanted, looking pleased and walking around the tables.

I sat a little straighter. Answer the questions? That did not sound so bad. I snatched a pencil and read the first thing on the sheet. *Your name here* the paper read. I put my name on the words. What a strange request! There was also a strange line next to the statement, but I did not pay that too much attention. That was not so bad. The next thing was a question. It asked:

1. *After George Washington chopped down the cherry tree in the myth, what did he say when his father asked him what happened?*

   A. *"The tree fell on it's own!"*
   B. *"I can tell a lie"*
   C. *"When I went outside, the tree was already like that!"*
   D. *"I can not tell a lie."*

I nudged Summer. "You just circle the correct answer?" I whispered. She snorted.

"Uh, yeah! Don't bother me, I'm almost done!" Summer went back to scribbling furiously. I moved on to the next question.

The test was really easy. Right in the middle of the test, though, someone farted. Really loud. It seemed louder than it actually was, because the room was so quiet. A few giggles followed. After I was done (which I was the first), I plopped my packet on Mrs. Zooka's desk. I sat back down and waited.

Ten minutes later (I was counting the time. What else was I supposed to do?), Mrs. Zooka called me to her desk, her face solemn for once. "You got all of the questions correct." She gave a small smile. "Congratulations." I smiled back.

"Thank you," I replied before returning to my seat. I stared at the wall, replaying my moment of success over and over again.

When the bell rang, Summer and I walked out of the classroom, returned papers in hand. Summer groaned. "C! This is C+ work!" she complained, showing the test to me for less than a second before taking it away again. "I made sure I studied hard enough to get a C+! *Not* a C! What's the matter with her?! I mean, she knows how much I studied

for this, and not even a plus! It just makes me so…
AAARGH!" Summer growled, her hands clenched
into fists. We put our things in our lockers and
trudged to class.

☆ ☆ ☆

Mr. Wallstone started talking about cells,
which I already knew, so I stared at the wall.

I answered some compellingly easy questions
Mr. Wallstone asked during class, trying to distract
myself from the boredom I was slowly drawing
closer too.

Finally class was over, and my spirits renewed
knowing a game was coming with the next class.

CHAPTER 15

B efore I walked into the dressing room, Mr. Elk popped some clothes into my hands. Everyone started changing their clothes, so I changed too. Everybody flooded out of the changing rooms, talking. Mr. Elk blasted his whistle, and everyone stopped chattering.

"Okay, today we're gonna to play *Tug-O-War*!" Mr. Elk gestured to a rope in the center of the room, then continued. "The rules are simple. Tug the rope till your team gets that ribbon in the middle." He stepped to the side so we could see the ribbon. "The team who gets to the ribbon first wins! Any questions?" No hands were raised. "Good. Today we'll use captains. Summer, Maddie, please do the honors." Summer and Maddie stepped in front of the gym class.

"I'll go first!" Maddie declared as she analyzed everyone. "I choose... Marco." Someone who looked strong stepped behind Maddie.

"Luna," Summer countered.

"Janice," Maddie stated smugly. They chose, until there was only one person left. Lucas. He was on our team.

"Pick your sides!" Mr. Elk called out. Each team went to a side of the rope. The shiny blue ribbon glittered. I wanted that ribbon. I. Wanted. That. Ribbon. "Ready. Set. Gooo…" Some people from both sides started pulling. "…ooat." They stopped tugging, realising their mistake, while Mr. Elk laughed. "Got ya. Ready. Set. Gooo…" No one moved. "…ooo…" No one flinched. "…gert. Man! Almost. Ready. Set. GO!"

We started yanking with all of our might, working like a team. Except for me. I just touched the rope, not wanting my "abnormal" strength to win this for us. Only if it was an emergency. The rope was moving at a rapid pace in our hands. Shouts of joy and groans of exertion surrounded me. Summer had touched the blue ribbon!

We played again, but this time they had Mr. Elk on their team. They *almost* won. I saved us.

We played again and again, each time losing a player, but with me, saving us every time, we could not possibly lose. Then Mr. Elk took *me* off the team. Four people to ten, we were going to lose. And we did. But the score was eight to one. We still won the overall game. Everyone said,

"Good Game" to each other; then we retired to the dressing rooms, and we changed into our regular clothes.

"That was a *great* game," Summer said, adjusting her shirt.

"Mmhmm," I answered, waiting for her to finish getting dressed. Summer tied her shoes. My feet were hurting so bad; I needed to take them off soon.

"Okay, let's go." Summer stood up. We start walking. "Hey, do you want to... nah, nevermind, you wouldn't like it," she said. I stopped.

"Like what?" I asked.

"Nothing," Summer said, trying to hide her smile. I sighed.

"Summer," I said warningly.

"Oh, alright. I was just going to super-glue Vortex's drawers shut. No big deal." Summer sounded casual, like she did this every day. She probably did. "So... you want to come?" Summer asked eagerly, like a wolf wanting its prey. "During free period? *Please?*" she begged.

"Fine." What harm could it do?

CHAPTER 16

We sat in our seats *just* as the bell rang. Mr. Mongar came in and made a beeline for me. "Did you do your homework, Moon?" he sneered.

"No-" Mr. Mongar did not let me finish.

"Ha!" Mr. Mongar sucked in a breath like he was going to speak. Before he could start, I cut in.

"You did not give us homework," I said quickly.

"Must have forgotten," he mumbled. "Well, class, we are now going to draw or finish another copy of your vampire. Lucas, Maddie, pass out paper. Everyone else, when you get your papers, start drawing."

Mr. Mongar gave Lucas one stack of papers, and Maddie another. Maddie passed out the blank sheets of paper, while Lucas handed out our drawings from yesterday. When I got my blank paper, I started drawing Mr. Mongar's version of the vampires. I was half finished with the face when Lucas passed by. I kept working. When Mr. Mongar came by, I was finally at the waist.

"That's worse than your last one," he spat. "Vampires are supposed to be super strong and super fast! Where are the muscles?" Then he sighed. "Then again, natural talent is born, not made. Like me. I am a natural," he sneered. Mr. Mongar turned away to criticize someone else. I kept drawing.

Every once in a while, Mr. Mongar would check my work and denounce it ("That eye is terrible! Look at that line, it's out of place!"), and when he could not find anything else to complain about, he would go away, returning ten minutes to complain about the same things.

Amazingly, I got through it. I had my copy of Eva and two "acceptable" vampires. I also had no homework. The bell rang, and I dragged myself out of class, relieved it was finally over.

☆ ☆ ☆

As I put my things in my locker, I heard voices. Two *very* familiar voices. I tapped Summer on the shoulder before I could change my mind.

"Hm?" she questioned.

"I think I… left something back in…" *Whose classroom was nearest to the voices? Mr. Mongar. Oh man. This was bad.* "Mr. Mongar's classroom," I finished.

"Oh-kay," Summer said suspiciously. "If you say so."

I ran (like Summer) cautiously towards the room. The quiet voices greeted me in the hallway.

"-guessing It came here, to fit in, but we don't know how long It's been studying or known about this." Mr. Shrude.

"Well there's a strange one in my class, I'll give you that. Drew what looked like your wi-" Mr. Shrude coughed. Mr. Mongar went on. "Er... Little Helper.

"Hmm, that's strange. Keep an eye out, okay? It could change the world... for our benefit of course. Well, see you later."

The door opened and I sprinted (my way) to the cafeteria. I arrived at the door panting. After I regained my composure, I opened the door and stepped inside.

☆☆☆

I found Summer and sat beside her without getting any food. I was still breathing heavily. Summer realized I was next to her.

"What happened?" she asked. "Did he chase you out?" I shrugged my shoulders.

"I barely had enough time to grab my things?" I said, a question in my voice. Summer went back to eating her food. "So... what do you do at a sleepover?" I asked.

"Of course you wouldn't know," Summer said under her breath. "Well, a sleepover is when-"

I saw Mr. Shrude's hand.

"Duck!" I said as I pushed Summer and I under the table. Mr. Shrude came into full view, scanning the tables, looking for *me*. His gaze lingered on Summers' ownerless tray for a second before moving on.

"What's going on?" Summer whispered.

"Trust me," I breathed back.

Eventually Mr. Shrude left. I waited a few moments before letting Summer back up, and a few more before I climbed up. Summer gave me a look of confusion, but did not mention it again.

After what had happened, Summer lost her appetite. "Come on, let's glue Vortex's cabinet drawers shut." Summer put her food in the trash and her tray in the dirty tray pile.

CHAPTER 17

Nurse Vortex, as usual, was asleep. We snuck in quietly, darting behind the supply cabinets. Her junk, from yesterday, was cluttered around her desk. Every breath, her four chairs creaked. We creeped up to her table.

"Okay," Summer whispered. "You open the drawers, and when I tell you to close them, you close them. Understood?" I nodded. "And... open!" Summer took off the cap to the super-glue as I started opening the cabinets. Summer squirted a line of super-glue on the part where the desk connects with the drawer. As soon as she finished, I closed that one. And the next. And the one after that. After a while, I had to stop shutting drawers and start opening new ones. Soon, we were done. Summer shut the last drawer with a loud *BANG!* and said "Done! Now let's get out of here before Vortex wakes up."

"Who? You mean little old me?" a voice said from beside us. Summer and I slowly turned to face Nurse Vortex. I was about to say little was not even close to accurate. Then I thought again. We were already in enough trouble. "I finally caught you troublemakers. Oh, Luna! Since you are here, we are going to get you to the hospital once and for all!"

Without thinking, I scooped Summer up in my arms and ran. I would *not* go back to *The Building*. Summer looked shocked, but I kept plowing ahead. As we blew past the front doors, Summer snapped out of her trance.

"Wha... you... run... punch..." Summer clearly could not say anymore. I ran to my alley, and put her down. "Okay, what's going on?" Summer demanded. "I mean, super strength, super speed, that evil one second look you gave Maddie, the chocolate! And what was that about going to the hospital? You said she was doing a full body inspection! I demand a full explanation NOW!" Summer stomped her foot, her face twisted with fury. We both shivered a little in the frigid air.

"Um..." *How do I explain this?* I could not do it the simple way, so I guess I would have to start from the beginning. "Well, I lived in this... orphanage."

"Which orphanage?" Summer asked eagerly, probably excited she was getting answers.

"Please, just let me talk. It is hard enough as it is." I waited for her reply. Summer did not talk, so I went on. "It was not really an orphanage, because there were no other kids…"

I explained my old life. The horrible tests, Mr. Shrude, and Eva, who was like a mother to me. I told Summer about the last Disaster-Master, the conversation, and the strange visit from Ivy. I told her about my discoveries on the world in the sunlight, and the first time I saw her. I told Summer my daring escape, and about the last few days. How I felt when we met and I was intro-duced to humor for the first time. I told her every-thing. Even the conversation I eavesdropped… er… overheard with Mr. Shrude and Mr. Mongar. Summer nodded when I was finished. I took off my socks and shoes and sighed in relief.

"Wow," Summer said, staring at me. "Tha-that's a lot to take in." Then her face lit up. "It's like a big adventure story! I've always wanted to be in one! You're so lucky!" I laughed bitterly.

"Yes, if you mean by 'lucky' getting chased by someone who knows your greatest weaknesses and strengths, who could make your life miserable by the flick of his wrists!" Summers' brightly lit face dimmed at my remark.

"Uhh… maybe you're not so lucky. So… how can I help?" she offered. I did not know what to do, but I had a question I really wanted answered.

"I guess… we could start by finding out who or what I am." Silence. We both thought, thinking in those frozen moments. Summer came up with something first.

"We could go where it all started?" she suggested. No. I was not going to go back there for a long time.

"Not unless we have too," I replied. Summer sighed.

"Yeah, I guess I see why that's a bad idea. They could catch you, and there are a lot of bad memories there for you." I then asked Summer a question I really wanted to know and was sure she could answer.

"Summer, when we first met, your eyes looked like they were going to pop out of your head. Why? Did I look strange?"

"Was I that obvious?" she asked. I nodded. Summer sighed. "Okay. Well—"

A kid who looked about our age in black clothing wearing a black mask jumped from one rooftop to another above us. I shot up out of my standing position. Summer slowly stood up beside me.

"What?" she whispered anxiously.

"Somebody is trying to spy on us. Let's find out who it is," I said. I picked Summer up and carried her as I started climbing the building the person jumped onto. Once we reached the top, I set her back on her feet. She let out a small "oof."

Summer and I kept low, the cars blaring in the streets around us, chasing the kid. "Couldn't you just use your super speed thingy?" Summer asked as she gulped for air. "I mean, the kid might already know. And if he doesn't, he's not looking back at us anyway." The familiar agony of burning set in now that we were not in the shadowed alleyway.

"Fine. Hop on." I needed to find out if the kid knew my secret.

"Piggy-back ride!" Summer squealed as she jumped on my back. In the next millisecond we were right next to the kid. Slowing down, I snatched his sleeve. The boy yelped, then tried to move faster. I easily sayed in pace with the stranger. The kid started panting, slowed down, then stopped completely.

"Okay, okay, you caught me." The intruder faced us. The mask was made so you could only see the eyes and some skin near the eyes. The same eyes of the stranger from the rooftop, in the bushes.

"Who are you?" I asked while Summer jumped off my back.

"Take off the mask, wanna-be Ninja," Summer demanded. "News Flash! If you wear black in the DAYTIME we can still SEE you!" The kid took off the mask and put his hands in the air. It was...

"Lucas?" I said, shocked.

"So... is it true?" Lucas asked sheepishly. Seeing my horrified face, he set up an excuse. "Well, I was just passing by and... and I heard, like, something about the Disaster-Master and fighting some lions? So, then, well, I was interested... er... *tired*, yeah, tired, so I sat down to rest and couldn't help overhearing-"

"Eavesdropping," Summer interrupted. I felt like punching something. Now two people knew my secret?

"Yes," I said regretfully. "It is true. And if you tell anyone, I will track you down." I was so stupid. Telling Summer in an alley where anyone could have overheard!

"I-I won't tell anyone. A-and maybe I could help too? I'm really good with computers and stuff."

"Fine! You can help," I said, sighing. Lucas turned to leave. "But before you go," I asked, "could you tell me what a Ninja is?"

CHAPTER 18

Later that evening, I knocked on the door of The Chocolate Shop. Summer was beside me, and we were a couple minutes early for the sleepover. We had come straight from school. Mrs. Vinely opened the door with a big smile on her face.

"Come in, come in," Mrs. Vinely said as she ushered us into the store. The smell of chocolate wafted through the air. Counters and shelves were filled with cookies, cakes, and even chocolate bars. Fudge and chocolate ice-cream showed through the clear refrigerator doors. The oven light was on, showing the cooking brownies. Bowls were filled up to the brim with batter. Jars were bursting with different kinds of chocolate chips. White chocolate, dark chocolate. Chocolate chip pancakes, chocolate chip muffins. Anything that had chocolate in it, you could find in this shop.

"Summer, take your friend upstairs to the living room and I'll send up some refreshments. Maddie and Janice should be here soon," Summer's mom said.

The smell of all that chocolate made me actually drool. It pulled me like a magnet, and I wanted to stuff it all in my mouth. Summer basically dragged me up the brown stairs, and showed me to a big room. In the center of the room there was a huge circular beige carpet. Chestnut couches were pushed off towards the side. A cinnamon table joined the couches. The walls gleamed a bright, clean white. A television sat on a wall.

As Summer and I sat down in the center of the soft carpet, Mrs. Vinely came up the stairs with her chocolate splattered apron. Summer's younger sister trailing behind Mrs. Vinely, who carried a giant platter of treats. Behind them Janice carried a gallon of chocolate milk, and Maddie carried four glasses. They set the refreshments down between Summer and me. I snagged some cookies, and poured myself some chocolate milk. We scooted back to make room for Janice and Maddie. Mrs. Vinely walked toward the stairs with elegance.

"Have a good time girls!" she called behind her. Anna tried to sit with us, but Summer scowled at her sister.

"Go away Anna! You're being so annoying," Summer growled. Anna crossed her arms.

"Why do you get all the snacks and I get none? I wanna stay up here! Besides, you don't have to work! It's not fair, so I'm staying." Anna plopped down beside us awkwardly. Summer sucked in a deep breath.

"MOOOOMM! ANNA'S BOTHERING US!" she hollered.

"AM NOT!" Anna yelled back.

"ARE TOO!" They kept yelling at each other until Summer's mom hollered back up the stairs.

"ANNA, LEAVE YOUR SISTER ALONE! THE BROWNIES ARE BURNING!"

Anna pouted, and flounced downstairs.

"So what should we do first?" Maddie grumbled as she readjusted her seat, eyeing me as I snatched another chocolate chip cookie... or three.

"Cheer up," Summer said, swatting Maddie playfully.

"Well? What are we going to do?" Janice asked.

"How about *Truth or Dare*?" Summer replied.

"Whatever," Maddie said, nibbling a cookie.

"How do you play *Truth or Dare*?" I asked timidly, reaching for another cookie, and emptying my glass of chocolate milk. I poured myself another. Summer and and Janice explained the game while Maddie grumbled in the background about me being stupid and not knowing about the simplest things.

We played a few games then started talking about boys. I did not know anything about this topic, so I was uncomfortable, but I kept silent. There were only two cookies left on the plate, and since I wasn't talking, I decided I should eat them. Maddie went to reach for a cookie, but seeing there were none, she glowered at me.

"You ate the whole plate," she hissed. I shrugged. Maddie scowled and went to refill her chocolate milk. There wasn't any left either. She gasped. "And drank all the milk!"

I smiled at her awkwardly, but not apologetically. It was not my fault—they were really good! It was not like I could ever resist chocolate.

Janice and Summer started probing Maddie about a boy she liked, and in her embarrassment, she soon forgot about the cookies. The doorbell rang. Since I was not paying attention to the "boy talk" thing, I listened to Mrs. Vinely opening the door. Had Summer invited more people?

"Oh, Hi! Can I help you?" Mrs. Vinely said, startled. *So, if these people were not guests, who were they?*

"Hello. Are you the owner of The Chocolate Shop?" said a deep male voice. "I believe a child —"

CHAPTER 18

A female voice interrupted. "We think our daughter is here. Luna? Luna Moon."

CHAPTER 19

My body went rigid at the sound of those voices. I panicked. Summer, sitting across from me, was the first to notice. She jumped up.

"Excuse me, I have to use the bathroom," she said hurriedly. Summer ran out of the room as fast as she could go. Janice and Maddie kept chatting. I heard Summer pick up a phone and dialed a number in the room next to us.

Downstairs Mrs. Vinely offered the two people who walked through the door some sweets. They kept declining. One of the people was Mr. Shrude. I knew by his recognizable voice. The other person's footsteps sounded a bit too light to be a normal human. Eva? Possible.

It was dark outside. I was excited and nervous at seeing Eva again. Maybe she would explain everything to me. Then again, she helped hold me captive. I pushed these thoughts away and focused on the conversation Summer was having with the person on the phone.

"-don't know what happened. She just tensed up and her eyes went wide with fear," Summer said. The phone started talking.

"I'll head over and keep a lookout for—"

Pounding footsteps came from the stairs.

"I gotta go," Summer rushed as she hung up on Lucas. Summer dashed into the room, and sat down right as *they* came in. I did not turn to face them. I already knew who they were.

"Hello, Luna." I could hear the cruel smile in his voice.

"Girls, we hate to interrupt, but we just received news from our doctor that our daughter Luna needs emergency surgery," Eva's soothing voice explained. "My husband"—Eva almost choked on the word—"says we have to take her to the hospital *right now.*"

The girls all looked concerned. Summer, most of all. "Would you girls like to ride over to the hospital with her?"

I tried to force a pleading message to Summer out of my eyes. *No! No! Say no!* But in the end it would not matter. They would take her and maybe the other girls by force eventually. Like they were going to have to take me. And they knew it.

"Summer?" Mrs. Vinely asked. Summer received my mental message.

"Thank you for offering, but no thanks," Summer said politely, glancing over at Maddie and Janice. "I need to stay here with my other guests."

"Well, too bad. Luna sure is going to miss you. Come on, Luna," Mr. Shrude said forcefully to me. I did not move. "Come on, Luna," he growled. Mr. Shrude lowered his voice so only Eva and I could hear him. "Luna, when we get back, it's going to be far worse than you had in the past. Eva!" Mr. Shrude ordered in his normal volume. Eva, against my best efforts, forced me to my feet and hesitantly shoved me down the steps and through the door with Mr. Shrude close behind.

There were two soldiers dressed as paramedics outside the doorway. A large, armored truck clumsily painted white and red was parked in the middle of the street, with a large red siren hooked on the top. Four other men dressed as medical workers brought out a stretcher. "Restrain It!" Mr. Shude demanded them. "We'll get the other girl later. It's almost time for my favorite game. A game called Torture 'Terrogation."

The soldiers— er, "paramedics," dropped the stretcher next to me, and forced me to lie on it. There were restraints for each of my four limbs, all of which I could not break; Mr. Shrude had tested it out on me when I was still living in

The Building. The fake paramedics flanked out, covering my every side. Eva was permitted to fasten the restraints, as she was the only one who could both hold me down and fasten them safely. Through the soldiers, I thought I saw someone wearing black on the roof. He quickly ducked down when he saw me looking. *Was that... Lucas?*

Eva stepped away as soon as she'd finished all four, and two of the fake paramedics lifted one side of the stretcher between them while Eva lifted the other, dragging me to the armored truck disguised as an ambulance. The others surrounded us, and one went to start the truck. They marched like a parade, even though there were only a few of us. I wondered what people would think when they saw us. People stopped and stared, but they did not interfere. And why would they? They thought these people were going to help me, not hurt me.

My eyes burned, and I closed them. I could not believe I had let myself be captured! Eva's side of the stretcher dipped for a moment, before evening out again. She would not have dropped the stretcher unless she wanted something; she was too strong for that. I opened my eyes, and turned to look at her. Her gaze met mine, before dropping to the restraints, and meeting mine again. *What...?*

I shifted. *Wait— the fact that I could move meant my restraints were loose!* That was impossible; Eva was the strongest, fastest person I knew, even stronger and faster than me. Unless she purposely left them loose, and wanted me to escape. Her eyes flashed to my face once more as if to say *What are you waiting for?*

Without thinking, I jerked my arm and leg on the side of the soldiers towards the other side, wrenching the stretcher enough that the surprised soldiers dropped it. Eva dropped her side as well, almost at the same time. Eva subtly used her foot to tear open one of my arm restraints. Once that was free, I used that hand to rip open the rest of the bonds, and I ran.

I ran. I ran and ran like the night they found me missing. I hid in the woods, away from any open areas. Something like ten, twenty minutes later, someone in a black Nin, Nin... ja outfit joined me.

"So it is true," Lucas said, eyes wide. I am sure his mouth was open, but I could not be sure because the mask was covering it. "A-about how they're chasing you and stuff. If I had any doubts before, let me assure you, they're gone."

"How did you find me?" I asked.

"I'm a Ninja," he said. Lucas winked. He seated himself and started chatting away about how awesome this part of the fight was, and how amazing my "powers" were... I sat too and thought about nothing. I was vaguely aware of everything, taking everything in, but just thinking of nothing. A blank mind, a blank slate... Soon, too soon, it was dark.

"Can I have a piggy-back ride? Summer did," Lucas asked. "Besides, we're really far away and I'm tired from chasing you that far." I searched my memories for any recount of a "piggy-back ride."

"You mean that thing where you ride on my back? I guess." Lucas hopped on my back. I dashed at top speed back to The Chocolate Shop. I figured it was the last place they would look.

"Wheee..." Lucas's voice quietly trailed behind us. Not breaking stride, I ran up to The Chocolate Shop window, peeking into the store. Mrs. Vinely flitted around the store, preparing food. She looked unbothered, so hopefully that meant Mr. Shrude did not harass her anymore today.

I focused my hearing to try and see if Maddie and Janice were still there; from what I could hear, they were having a lot of fun upstairs.

My back felt a few pounds lighter, and a soft thud entered my ears from behind me. Lucas had dropped off my back.

"Are you going to be okay?" Lucas asked.

"I think so," I said. "It was not like they hurt me ... yet." Lucas was quiet for a moment, his forehead wrinkled as he thought.

"What if they come back? We need to make a plan," he said. "Let's go up and talk with Summer—"

"Maddie and Janice are still up there," I told him. "We were having a sleepover until Mr. Shrude tried to take me."

"Okay, well then let's get together tomorrow and brainstorm. I'll call Summer and let her know." Lucas smiled mischievously. "And we'll have our meeting at her house. Her mom makes the best food, and loves to host. I'm sure she won't mind." I grinned back at him. I would not say no to more chocolate.

CHAPTER 20

The next day, after school, we all walked to The Chocolate Shop together. True to his word, Lucas had called Summer the night before and filled her in.

Summer stopped us before we entered the store. "The key here," she told us, "is speed."

Lucas looked at her. "What are you talking about?"

She laughed nervously, sheepish. "I...maybe didn'ttellmymomyouwerecoming. But it's all right! Trust me," Summer said, setting her shoulders back. Lucas and I glanced at each other, uncertain. Summer took a deep breath, grabbed both our wrists, and yanked us inside. The door jangled.

"Hi mom we have a group project we'll be upstairs thankyouloveyou!" Summer called out as she pulled us quickly up the stairs.

"What—" her mom said, startled. We were already upstairs. "SUMMER!" Mrs. Vinely called out. We all froze. Was she mad?

"DO YOU WANT SNACKS?" Mrs. Vinely said instead. We all sagged, letting out breaths of relief.

"YES, PLEASE!" Lucas and I hollered back. Summer looked at me, considering.

"EXTRA CHOCOLATE PLEASE, MOM! THANKS!" Summer added. Dishes clanked as Mrs. Vinely prepared our food.

We all collapsed on the fluffy beige carpet in the living room. Lucas rummaged in his book-filled backpack before bringing out a pad of paper and a pen, flipping to a blank page and uncapping his pen.

"Before we can figure out how to avoid Mr. Shrude, we need to figure out why they want you," Lucas stated. "Luna, what can you do that normal people can't?"

"Well, I can..." I hesitated. What *could* I do that Summer and Lucas could not? Summer slapped a hand against her forehead.

"Ugh, I need to make sure Anna doesn't bother us. I *totally* forgot. And since I'm guessing you don't want her knowing about you," Summer sent a pointed look towards me, "I'm going to go downstairs and tell my mom to keep her away from us." Summer stood up and tromped down the stairs, and I heard her talk with her mom.

Lucas turned his attention back towards me. "So, Luna, what have you noticed?"

"Well, I can run five miles a second so I guess I can move faster than you guys. I can lift six tons, I can see, hear, and smell for around ten miles. I can survive a fight with a tiger. I can endure being dumped into a pool of super charged radioactive water. I don't really need to sleep. I can-"

Lucas gestured in a stop motion.

"I get it, I get it. So, we know you probably aren't human. Well, maybe you are, but not entirely." He tapped the pen against his lips, thinking. "You don't drink blood, do you?" Lucas asked anxiously, pointing the pen at me.

Before I could answer, Summer came back up the stairs with a tray of chocolate foods.

"Good news guys; Anna has to stay after school for some club or something, so she won't be bothering us unless you guys are staying here really late." She placed the tray down, and I snatched up a chocolate goodie. Lucas filled Summer in on what I just told him.

"I might have a theory," he added to the end of his explanation. "Once Luna answers my question, we can see if I'm right or not. Well, Luna? Or have you forgotten what I asked you?" His eyes turned on me. I swallowed my mouthful of chocolate goodness before answering him.

"Ew, no. Blood is gross. Mr. Shrude did make me interact with it though. I was seated in a chair in the Disaster-Master and there was a sponge full of blood. They made me squeeze out the blood." *I shuddered. That had felt nasty.* "I only ran off to wash the blood from my hand," I told him. Lucas sighed. I reached for another treat from the plate. When I looked down though, they were all gone. I sheepishly pulled my hand away. *Oops.*

"Well, then we can cross that off the list."

"Cross what?" Summer asked, pulling over some chairs.

"I thought she was some sort of vampire, like Mr. Mongar told us, because she's super fast and strong. But Luna said she didn't drink blood and she can go in the sun, so that's out. I have some other theories, but that one had the most evidence for it."

"I mean, I do think the sun hurts me. It is painful to be in direct sunlight," I interjected.

"Yeah, but if you were a vampire, you would've died at this point," Summer said. "Remember? Mongar said that the sun kills vampires. Maybe you just have some sort of really weird skin condition!" she tacked on.

We were quiet for a moment, thinking everything over. Lucas's eyes lit up.

"We could always Google it!" he exclaimed.

"What is Google?" I asked cluelessly. They both sighed.

CHAPTER 21

We were really busy the next few weeks, and strangely, no one bothered us—at school, or The Chocolate Shop. Summer and Lucas gave me lessons on how to be more human. At the same time, we were looking at creatures I could be on the Internet, doing all of this, while acting normal, which was quite a challenge. We also found out the hard way, as humans say, that I can eat food, as long as it has some chocolate in it. But, I never found out how Summer knew me and if Lucas was the strange brown/black eyes I saw. Once, Mrs. Marlock told me if I kept being smart then I would have to go into the Gifted Program. Since I didn't want to draw attention to myself, I dialed down how much "smartness" I showed. *Did that sound correct?* Anyway, in summary, we were busy and tired the whole few weeks.

My suspicions were getting higher and higher every minute someone didn't try to capture us, or had a mysterious conversation, or Mr. Shrude or Eva did not pass by. I was on high alert and very tense all the time. I kept moving around, or was it called pacing? Summer and Lucas said I was just paranoid, but I didn't let my guard down. Never in my life, even when I was battling solid holographic sword masters, was I ever this nervous.

Finally, something happened. I gasped. Behind me in the lunch line, Summer poked me in the side.

"What's wrong?" she whispered.

"It's something really suspicious," I whispered back. "They are not serving chocolate chip cookies anymore. That has to be a sign of hostility." Summer shook her head.

"Sadly, schools just do that. Once they gave us COLD chicken nuggets for WEEKS. You're just being paranoid. Relax," Summer said as we moved forward in the lunch line. "They haven't come for you in, what? Two months? They probably gave up. Or, better yet, forgot about you entirely. The government has more important stuff on its mind."

Even though those words weren't really reassuring, somehow I did start to relax. It was not until a whole week though, until I wound down fully.

"It is actually nice being relaxed," I said to Summer and Lucas on our way back from art class.

"Wait, so have you never been, you know, chill, before?" Lucas asked, interested. I thought back into my life.

"No, I don't think so," I replied as we pushed open the cafeteria doors. They pondered this as we got into line.

The regular lunch ladies were not there. Instead, there were big burly men wearing sunglasses, aprons, and hairnets. I didn't think much of it. I did not want to be paranoid.

At the end of the line the Lunchman asked me in a deep voice, "Luna, is it?"

"Huh?" I accidentally replied. Then the man did something with his hands. He made a movement, like what Summer and Lucas told me was a peace sign you make with your hands, or the number two.

Men poured out of nowhere, wearing sunglasses and tuxedos, pulling out guns. People screamed. Others shouted "Cool!" or "Awesome!!!" in the chaos. The Lunchmen behind the counter ripped off their hairnets and aprons, revealing they were dressed like the rest of the intruders. The Lunchmen also pulled out thin, slender guns. People in the army burst in too, their black and green uniform swirling together like a pattern. One of the green wearing people pulled out a bullhorn.

"Kids and teachers, please evacuate the building. My men will get you out safely. Unless of course you are-" He spit out the word with venom in it, like he wished he could avoid saying the word all together. "-that Monster. Please vacate the building quietly and calmly."

The men then started coming towards me. I heard gunshots. I was preoccupied ducking and diving to see if Summer and Lucas had stayed. Sometimes I crashed into walls, breaking off bits and pieces of it. The screaming faded. Most of the people must have gotten out and calmed down by now. I tried not to hurt the soldiers chasing me, but sometimes it was inevitable. I cringed and flinched at the groans of anguish and the cries of agony. Somewhere in the midst of all the fighting, ducking, and dodging, I felt a little prick on the heel of my foot. My shoes must have come off. I saw the moon, the stars and the night sky. *It was night already?* A gentle thud filled the room. The sky was spinning.

"Luna!" Summer's voice faintly called. Soft tickling things touched me all over. I felt like I had risen a few inches.

"Luna!" Lucas urgently whispered. *Why were they whispering? And what was so urgent?* Darkness enclosed me. I was in nothingness. I was nothing.

CHAPTER 22

I opened my eyes to see black. Slowly I sat up. Quiet crackling noises came from beneath me. Everything was spinning. *Was that normal? I was so stiff. Where was I? How long was I here? How did I get here?* I looked down to see snow white sheets on a bleached bed. I looked around.

Everything was white. The bed was white, the walls were white, even the pillow behind me was white. I looked up. The ceiling was a giant black hole. That was really all of the color here. The black, the white, and me. I started pacing the room. Lucas and Summer's voices haunted me. "Luna! Luna!" Their echoes were calling to me. I tried to distract myself. I hummed tuneless tunes. I braided my hair. I sang aloud "Twinkle, Twinkle Little Star" and the "ABC's." I even went back in my memories and tried to play out if someone said or did something differently. Anything really, to keep the voices at bay.

I was making up one of the many stories of why Summer recognized me, when a rope dropped from the inky darkness above. Someone followed the rope. Someone I have been dreading and expecting. My torturer. My executioner. My warden.

Mr. Shrude.

Two soldiers with dart guns followed. In the darts was a clearish, silvery liquid. Another white thing. Ugh. Mr. Shrude was the first one to speak.

"You can never escape us, Luna Moon. No matter how many times you escape, no matter where you go, we will always find you." A smug look was fitted on his face, like a hat he could wear. Escape had never crossed my mind, but neither had what he would do to me. *At the same time, what more could he do to me than he already has?*

"And, you are going to stay here until you willingly help me."

Okay, now that's a different situation. What was the use of surviving all Mr. Shrudes other tests if I was going to die of boredom? But, I also couldn't surrender to him. That would show I was weak. And, well, he and Eva taught me never to show weakness. At the same time, they also told me to obey them at all costs.

"Well?" he asked, that smug look never leaving his face.

"NO," I said firmly. His smile faltered.

"Well then," a forced smile took its place. "You are going to stay here." The guards, sensing dismissal, started climbing the rope. Mr. Shrude, when the soldiers were about halfway, latched himself on. "Call if you change your mind," he said, rising into the ceiling. His creepy laugh followed him like a swarm of flies.

I stayed in my room, smashing into walls, trying to climb the barrier, and basically trying to escape. A couple of hours later, a chocolate bar was dropped into my cell. I nibbled at it, starved as I was, to preserve it as long as possible. When I finished, I went back to trying to escape. It felt like forever until the rope dropped down again. I sat on my bed, straight and tall, trying to look confident and as though I wasn't even tempted to take Mr. Shrude's offer. *But, if I did not, then how would I get out?* I found no escape so far, and I was not that creative, so I couldn't entertain myself forever. I was smart. Summer was the creative one. *Wait, I am a genius. Maybe I can outwit them.* I was definitely smart enough.

The guard yanked on the rope twice. I ran and started climbing the rope before their human brains could register what they were seeing, but my lack of chocolate made me slower. I estimated thirty and five tenths MPH. I was about halfway and could see the rim. I was in either a huge hole, or a large bucket.

"Cut the rope!" Come on, come on, two-thirds of the way there! Just a little longer... *Snip.* They cut the rope, and both the cut rope and myself fell back down, into the hole. There went my escape. As I hit the floor, I saw Mr. Shrudes face was purple. *Whoa, human faces could change color?* His face was twisted and pulled in fury. Seeing me looking, he composed himself.

"Well?" he asked, knowing I remembered the question.

"NO." Thankfully, my voice did not shake.

"Fine. ROPE!" he called up to the rim. His face showed very *very* little of his fury. At least that was what I thought.

☆☆☆

It went on like this for two days. Every day I could see more of how angry Mr. Shrude was, and my will slowly crumbled like a decomposing leaf in the fall. After every "talk" and they went back up, and I got chocolate. I'm sure it was the same amount as before, but it felt like it was shrinking. Half starved, I prepared for the fourth visit.

CHAPTER 23

Mr. Shrude had something in his hands this time. Pieces of paper.

"I have a surprise for you!" he called, his triumphant grin like a bug. Not that I dislike bugs, they are very interesting to study. "We *invited* a guest and they graciously accepted." My breathing sped and my heartbeat accelerated at the word "guest." Who was this unlucky person? Friend or foe? "It's your little friend!" Mr. Shrude said joyfully, showing me the pictures. "Summer!" He laughed, like it was a joke Summer told him.

I did not pay attention to him. I stared, in awestruck horror, at the photograph. It looked like she was sleeping. She was laid out on the stone floor. The photograph was colorless, but I could tell she wasn't sleeping. She was... she was...

"Dead!" Mr. Shrude said gleefully. "Dead, dead, dead!" he said, smiling, laughing, jumping up and down.

Summer? Dead? No, i-it couldn't be! Summer, sweet, funny, easy-going Summer? A shrill shriek of the most heart-struck pain filled the room. *What were they doing to that poor person? And how was it filling the room?* I was choking, drowning, suffocating. The siren wail grew louder. Mr. Shrude and his "bodyguards" looked at me, their expressions surprised. Oh. That siren wail shriek was me. I just then noticed the wet drops streaking down my cheeks. Were those... tears?

"Well," Mr. Shrude said, clearly ruffled. "Will you take my offer?" *What was the point of resisting if one of my pillars was gone?* I still had Lucas I guess, but I needed a girl. A girl to kind of understand what I am going through. A girl to make me laugh, to help me see the bright spots in the hard times.

"Fine," I whispered almost inaudibly, shocked with myself. "Just give me more chocolate."

Mr. Shrude's smile was so big it filled the room. It filled my nose, my eyes, my mind, my lungs. I was suffocating again.

"Great! The tests start tomorrow." Then he called up to the ceiling. "Lennox, unload the truck!" It started raining chocolate bars. Twix, Milky Way, 3 Musketeers. Hershey's, Snickers, and Butterfingers. A whole pile of chocolate. A whole mound of chocolate. A whole *mountain* of chocolate. I inhaled. Mmmm. My mouth was watering. But I restrained myself, waiting for

Mr. Shrude to leave me so he would not see me eat like a savage animal. "See you tomorrow!" he called with victory as the rope slowly pulled him up.

It was too slow. I was afraid I was going to snap right there. It was not that I was afraid of killing Mr. Shrude that I restrained, oh no, I wanted to leave him bloodied and bruised right there on the floor. It was because I didn't want him to see his success in starving me. To see his gloating grin of triumph. Finally, after one hundred and twenty four and sixty two hundredths *LONG* seconds, he was out of the hole. And, in less than five minutes, all that chocolate was gone.

I put all the licked clean wrappers in a big pile, right where Mr. Shrude would stand tomorrow. It was a small punishment for what he did, but it was all I could do. My stomach was grateful to be full. It was celebrating. But my mind was mourning. My mind was saying *"Stop celebrating!"* but my stomach would not listen. Not just my stomach, but my whole body. It was buzzing with electricity. My muscles wanted to get moving, to lift something, to run! My nerves were aching to see, touch, taste, hear, and smell. But, instead of listening to my body's wants, I sat on my bed, clasped my hands together, and grieved for Summer.

CHAPTER 24

I stayed like that until Mr. Shrude came down, but he didn't step on the wrappers like I had intended. Of course my eyes were still closed, but I didn't hear crunching sounds like leaves underfoot in autumn.

"Well, ready for some tests today? We have a lot to catch up on!" Mr. Shrude said cheerily. I opened my eyes. "Of course, we'll have to put this on first, just for extra precautions." Mr. Shrude was wearing his usual tuxo… that is the short version of saying tuxedo, right? Mr. Shrude looked around. "Note to self," he muttered, eyeing the pile. "get Bob to clean this mess. Why are all of the janitors named Bob?"

Then, my dreaded tracker made its appearance. It dropped from the sky, and when it hit the ground, it made a loud *CLANG!* Two men slid down after it. Mr. Shrude took out the tiny silver key. "Just extra precautions," he repeated as the two strong (for humans) men barely lifted it off the floor.

Reluctantly, I held out my arm. Placing the band on my wrist and out of breath, they quickly hurried away from me, startled. I don't know why. They already knew about my "abnormal" strength. Mr. Shrude came over and, sadly, locked it. There goes my freedom. Not like I had much hope in this wretched place.

"Alrighty!" said Mr. Shrude, way too cheerful for my mood. "Let's do this! Albert, take the key, and put it in the safe. Okay?" Mr. Shrude handed "Albert" the key, which Albert put in his pocket. Then he started climbing the rope. "As for you," Mr. Shude said, turning toward me. "Well, we have a lot of tests to do, don't we?"

☆☆☆

I felt like a prisoner. Probably because I know what I was missing out on now. I felt like if I did a wrong move, I would be whipped like I was one of those horses in a chariot race. Things I had never felt before walking this hall. There was not much to tell. I got tortured, tortured, and tortured some more. I ran, lifted weights, and killed imprisoned animals who were probably treated better than me. Despair settled on my shoulders like a flock of ravens. I wanted to be free from killing. I felt...

ashamed, every time I helped him. Downtrodden from helping him again, I heard voices.

"Luna!" whispered a girl's voice. I banished it from my mind. I was imagining it.

"Luna!" whispered a boy. *They couldn't be here!* Instead of staring at my bare feet, my head perked up. I looked around, as fast as I could go, so the guards surrounding me wouldn't be suspicious and tell Mr. Shrude. When I looked at the doorway, I caught sight of a black sneaker before it disappeared. Lucas was here! I could not call back, but... I turned my head away so the soldiers wouldn't look at the doorway. I tapped the nearest guard on the soldier.

"Hey! I have to use the bathroom." The soldier's face reddened at my statement, then he went up and told Mr. Shrude. Mr. Shrude sighed, then signaled for us to stop.

"Fine! If you have to," Mr. Shrude snapped, clearly annoyed. "You two, go with her." He pointed at two soldiers. We walked down the familiar hallways.

When Mr. Shrude was far enough away, I easily overpowered the soldiers and knocked them out. I cocked my ears and listened for footsteps and people breathing. I knew where I was. My old room was near here. All I could hear was the two people next to me, their heartbeats, and their steady, even breathing.

Wait... No, just a mouse. I guess I'll have to search for them on my own. Quickly, I stored the two men in my old room. Nothing had changed much, except the clothes I had left behind were sprawled across the bed. Swiftly, I looked through the bathroom and, I shuddered, the Disaster-Master. Nothing.

I then decided I should probably trust my nose instead. I took a deep breath through my nose. Summers' chocolatey scent somehow mingled with Lucas's deep smell of pulpy books. I filled my nostrils with the scents. I followed the trail they had left behind with their scents. Once or twice I was almost seen by guards, but I snuck past them. I didn't have much time left. If I did not come back with the soldiers soon, Mr. Shrude would be suspicious.

Soon, the scents confused me. Four fresh scents lingered. Two were the guards. The other two were Summer and Lucas. Then all of the scents mixed together. Suddenly, an outraged cry reached my ears. The speakers above me crackled.

"Luna," said a sickly sweet voice, "I have your friend." The speakers growled in Mr. Shrudes voice. I flinched. "Come here, or he *WILL* suffer consequences." The faint crackling disappeared along with Mr. Shrudes voice. *I won't let him take Lucas from me too.* I sprinted into the Disaster-Master, the only room (that I know of) with speakers and a broadcasting system, but did not see Lucas anywhere. The locks clicked shut. I was trapped in the Disaster-Master.

CHAPTER 25

"Well, let's see what we have for you today."
Mr. Shrude was behind the controls,
alone. Who was this man, telling me what to
do? This man had kept me captive, torturing me,
tormenting me, only for his benefit. This man
before me was a sniveling coward. My rage flared.
A white hot fire burned inside me. But somehow,
I dampened it. Somehow, I kept my cool.

"Yes. Let's see," I spat. Mr. Shrude looked startled. Was it because he heard the venom in my
voice as well as I could? Was it because he could
feel my anger sizzling in the air? Or was it because
he didn't expect a reply? His fingers were crawling
towards The Button. The Button of My Misery,
that would start the Disaster-Master.

Before the fingers got even halfway, I did something that shocked me. Something I had not dared
before. I slammed into the thick panel separating
Mr. Shrude and me. Something that always sepa-
rated him from the danger I was facing. The plastic
glass shattered into a billion pieces. Mr. Shrude

looked scared and frightened. I almost smiled. I wanted to torture this man the way he tortured me. I wanted him to feel every ounce of misery he forced upon me. Then I realized what I was thinking. I... I was disgusted with myself. *Where were these new thoughts coming from? What was happening to me?*

Instead of hurting him like I wished too, I just said "*Never* underestimate me."

I hopped down from the control panel and sped off.

☆ ☆ ☆

Finally, I found Lucas near my old room. "You're okay!" we exclaimed at the same time.

"Luna, you almost gave Summer and me a heart attack," Lucas said. "I mean, being kidnapped like that —"

I cut him off.

"Wait, Summer is alive?" I asked him.

"Yeah. Summer and I followed the soldiers, sneaked in like Ninjas, and found you. Where have you been?!" Lucas asked.

"Here," I replied. Wasn't that obvious? He stared at me and raised his eyebrows. *Ohhhhh.*

"Human rhetorical remark thing?" I asked sheepishly. Lucas nodded.

"Summer! I found her!" he then called. Summer popped out from behind the hallway corner.

"Coming!" she shouted. Then she started mumbling. I really hope this wasn't about how well the buildings are built or the dents in the wall and it's about—

Summer caught sight of me. "Luna!" she shout-squealed. She sprinted as fast as she could (not very fast) towards me and gave me a hug. "We were so—"

"Worried, yes I know." I awkwardly hugged her back. The pocket of worry and sadness I had for Summer evaporated, and turned into relief. Summer was alive! My friend was alive! "We should probably get out of here before Mr. Shrude finds us," I suggested. Summer reluctantly let me go. Then that old, familiar, mischievous grin flitted onto her face.

"Well… if we need to get out of here *fast*… then could you give us a piggy back ride?"

"Fine," I replied, slightly annoyed. I didn't really want to give two people a piggy back ride. I crouched.

"Climb on," I said. Summer got on my back and Lucas got on hers. We sped off. I ran into my old room and hopped out the window, and I raced away into the woods.

As I was running (my speed), someone cut me off. Or should I say two someones. Ivy stood in front of me. The cool night air brushed against my skin. Behind Ivy was a big burly guy with sandy hair, brown eyes, and skin as pale as Ivy's and mine. I dropped Summer and Lucas off my back. "Ivy? What are you doing here?" I asked her, confused.

"Well, I had heard you escaped from *Them*," she obviously hated Mr. Shrude as much as I did, "then, I heard you were captured again so we came to rescue you. Apparently, you don't need it."

Ivy clearly had many resources, so she might know the answer to the question that was bugging me.

"Ivy?" I asked.

"Yeah?" she replied. I hesitated.

"What am I?" The question was innocent enough. Now Ivy hesitated.

"Luna," she said finally. "You're a vampire."

CPSIA information can be obtained
at www.ICGtesting.com
Printed in the USA
BVHW071206231121
622335BV00009B/275